咸寒英語有聲書 6
聖誕
禮物
The Gift of the Magi

# 目錄 *Contents*

# 目錄 Contents

歐亨利最感人的故事

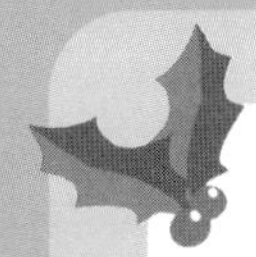

# 如何使用本書

本書包括兩個歐亨利的著名故事〈聖誕禮物〉、〈重新做人〉，是情境式的英語有聲書，一共有43段，以正常速度的英文呈現，反覆聽熟，讓你的英語會話及聽力更上層樓。

練習方法：請參閱《英文，非學好不可》一書。

# 意外的結局

## ——短篇小說之王歐亨利

人生似小說，往往有意外的結局，正是歐亨利短暫一生的寫照。

一則溫馨感人的故事，也許你也曾聽過：

「一對貧窮的年輕夫妻，男的叫吉姆，女的叫黛拉。他們家窮到什麼都沒有，唯有兩件引以爲傲的財富，一件是吉姆祖父留下來的傳家懷錶，另一件就是黛拉的一頭秀髮。他們彼此深愛著對方，當聖誕節來臨時，他們想盡辦法要送給對方最珍貴的禮物。

結果誰也料想不到，吉姆典當金錶，買下一支玳瑁做成的漂亮梳子送給黛拉。而黛拉竟剪下一頭秀髮賣掉，換來的錢買了一條精緻的白金短錶鏈，打算送給吉姆……」

### 短篇小說之王

這篇〈聖誕禮物〉（*The Gift of the Magi*，又譯〈三賢士的禮物〉），故事深刻而感人，無數讀者爭相傳誦，到後來，人們甚至忘記原作者是何許人。巴西作家保羅・科爾賀（Paulo

年輕時代的歐亨利（前排左）多才多藝，曾和朋友組成小樂團，他負責拉手風琴和彈吉他，在派對上表演。

Coelho）在他的暢銷作品《我坐在琵卓湖畔哭泣》最後一章也引用這個故事，佔了不少篇幅，對作者的名字卻隻字未提。

這故事的原創者是歐亨利（O. Henry），在現代文學史上有「短篇小說之王」（the master of the short story）的稱譽。

歐亨利小說的特色是，結局往往出乎讀者意料之外。故事

歐亨利人生最後幾年住在著名的卻爾希飯店。

歐亨利中年畫像。

一開始很平常，但經過縝密的布局，進行到最後，突然來個意想不到的「轉折」（twist），把讀者的閱讀神經拉到最高點，然後戛然而止，令人低迴深思。這種結局出人意外的「歐亨利式轉折」（O. Henry twist），他所寫的小說裡幾乎每一篇都有。我小時候看過的歐亨利短篇，而今依然歷歷如目呢！

有人問他，如何寫小說？他回答：「剛動筆時，我不一定會想到結尾，只讓情節隨著筆轉；有時候，則先想好結局，然後再鋪陳故事情節來配合結局。」

## 人生如戲，扮演過不同的角色

歐亨利其實是威廉．希德尼．波特（William Sidney Porter）的筆名，一八六二年九月十一日生於美國北卡羅萊納州，一九一〇年六月五日死於紐約時，疾病纏身，身上幾無分文，年未滿四十八歲。

圖最右邊是童年的歐亨利，最左邊是他哥哥薛爾。

歐亨利的雜貨店素描：一個男子手拿裝滿冰塊的瓶子，準備調製波本威士忌；後面三人正在玩牌。

歐亨利筆下的諷刺漫畫，描繪拎著毯製手提包的投機家飛來飛去。

22歲的歐亨利，在奧斯汀。

離世至今將一世紀，歐亨利寫的故事仍為讀者傳閱，翻譯成十幾種語言。一九六二年，蘇聯還為他出了一張紀念郵票。

歐亨利沒有正式上過學，因母親早逝，父親將他託付給祖母和姑媽照顧。姑媽開一家私塾，以英國小說家狄更斯（Charles Dickens）及司各特（Walter Scott）的小說為教材，他也跟著讀了許許多多的名著。十五歲他就一個人出外討生活，起先在叔叔的藥房裡實習，拿到藥劑師執照，餘暇還幫鎮上的居民畫素描和漫畫。

一八八四年他二十二歲，全家遷至德州（Texas）首府奧斯汀（Austin）。一八九三年至一八九五年間，歐亨利及家人住在奧斯汀東第五街四○九號，這座安女王風格（Queen Anne Style）的木造房子，如今已改設歐亨利紀念館，陳列他遺留的一些物品。你可以看到當年他伏案寫作的桌子，以及那張也許是引發他寫〈聖誕禮物〉靈感的椅子。一景一物，讓讀者一瞥二十世紀初，作者在世時的美國中產階級生活樣貌。

歐亨利可說是奧斯汀有史以來最出名的人物。

定居奧斯汀的十三年間，歐亨利從事過多種不同的行業：在牧場幹活、看雜貨店、持有牌照的藥劑師、地政繪圖員、銀行出納員、記者，他所經歷過的生活後來都一一融入他的筆

歐亨利在奧斯汀的故居，一如普通人的住家，目前已成立紀念館。（黃健敏 攝）

下。在一八九七年最後離開德州之前，歐亨利出版了第一部短篇小說集《火山熔岩谷奇蹟》（*The Miracle at Lava Canyon*）。

當年，由於女方家長不贊成婚事，他便和女友艾索兒（Athol）相偕私奔。起先，他在奧斯汀的第一國民銀行擔任出納員，幾年後離職，創立一本幽默雜誌，但銷售量很差；他也為《休士頓每日郵報》（*Houston Daily Post*）撰寫專欄。這時，他的厄運開始降臨。

歐亨利早逝的原配艾索兒。

## 從人生最低點開始爬格子

當他辭去職務幾個月後，第一國民銀行竟以盜用公款的名義向法院控告歐亨利，他雖極力否認，但事實真相如何，後人

歐亨利曾在第一國民銀行擔任出納員，因挪用公款惹上牢獄之災。

已不得而知。歐亨利沒有到奧斯汀投案，卻試圖逃跑，甚至跑到中美洲宏都拉斯（Honduras），後因妻子生病才悄然返國，被關入監牢三年餘，出獄時已近四十歲了。

人生的最低點，卻也是他另一人生的開端。身繫牢獄三年多，妻子病逝，為了撫養唯一的女兒，他開始爬格子，以筆名發表了十來個短篇小說賺稿費，引起讀者爭相傳閱，卻無人知道他是個囚犯。

他為自己取了「歐亨利」的筆名。這個名字，據說是來自他家的那隻貓，他經常喊牠：「Oh, Henry！」（哦，亨利！）；也有人說是法國藥學家 Eteinne-Ossian Henry 的名字縮寫，因為歐亨利在牢裡負責藥房的業務。

而諷刺的是，當年審判歐亨利的地點：奧斯汀市科羅拉多街六〇一號四〇四室（Room 404, 601 Colorado Street,

1895年，歐亨利與妻女合影，兩年後妻子便離開人世。

歐亨利的女兒，攝於1910年，父親病逝前不久。

歐亨利塑像。

Austin)，如今竟改名為「歐亨利廳」(O. Henry Hall)。

歐亨利在世的時候已經是很受歡迎的作家了，但沒有一個人真正認識他。由於擔心引人注意，讓其他犯人認出他的臉，直到死前，他堅持不曝光，不肯將本人照片公開亮相，也從不在公眾場合露面。連接受記者訪問時，也只同意以速寫畫的方式刊在報章雜誌上。離開人世時，僅留最後遺言：「把燈打亮，我不想在黑暗中回家。」(Turn up the lights.－I don't want to go home in the dark.)

## 人生的結局，誰也料不定

說到德州奧斯汀這地方，讓我想起一個人——從前曾經住過我家的一個台灣清華大學物理系男生，那時我才唸國一，他常帶著我唱校園名歌、彈吉他，騎摩托車載我到城隍廟吃貢丸湯。平日，見他一付懶懶散漫的德性，難得用功唸書。

「像他那樣愛打混的傢伙，如果能夠出國唸書，那全台灣的學生都可以上哈佛了！」我記得他的同學曾在背後議論他。

沒想到這個男生一畢了業，當兵被派到鳥不生蛋的外島東

17歲的歐亨利，撐日本洋傘，持手杖，作舞台打扮。

引，天天看到的，除了海還是海，閒著沒事，他只好K書打發時間。一年十個月的預官役竟成了他的修練期，以高分考過托福和GRE，彌補了大學的爛成績，先申請到奧勒岡大學（University of Oregon）唸碩士學位，然後跌破眾人眼鏡，他竟以優異的研究所成績進入排名頂尖的史丹佛大學（Stanford University），一路唸到博士，如今已在德州大學奧斯汀分校（University of Texas at Austin）擔任物理系副教授。

今日非昨，人生的結局，誰也料不定。誰說一試定終身，一如歐亨利的小說，往往出現意外！

## 筆下充滿「反諷」意味

歐亨利的故事以現實人生為背景，主角都是他所見過的平凡人物。他共寫了二百五十篇短篇小說，大部分是在一九〇二年到一九一〇他逝世那年期間寫的。他一度替《紐約世界報》（*New York World*）寫小說，每星期一篇，每篇一百元，五十二個星期沒有中斷。那八年他都住在紐約，以他周圍的眾生為題材，描寫社會名流、女店員、計程車司機、

歐亨利曾經坐過牢，他擔心被其他犯人認出，堅持不曝光，連接受記者採訪時，也只同意以速寫畫的方式刊在報章雜誌上。

熨斗大樓——歐亨利時代的摩天樓，坐落於紐約百老匯及第五街之間。

1901年，紐約第六街的高架鐵道。

窮畫家、流浪漢、警察、小偷、劫匪等。他說：「人類情緒的每一種表現，都是小說的材料。」

他一直留在紐約，理由是：「聽不到高架鐵道的聲音，又怎麼能寫作呢？」

每一個讀者都能深深感受他筆下的「反諷」（irony）意味。“irony”這個字源自希臘喜劇角色「Eiron」，屢次以機智鬥敗了自我膨脹的另一角色「Alazon」。十六世紀之後，「反諷」延伸為不用正面的、直接的發言，而是以婉轉的、隱晦的文字，譏刺、點化、感染讀者，使讀者醒悟，進而對事實有公正、客觀及深入了解事件表相，從而接受隱藏在事件背後的真相。

以歐亨利最著名的〈聖誕禮物〉為例，這對夫妻如此為對方著想，寧願犧牲彼此最珍貴的東西來換取對方所愛，到頭來

卻兩頭空；慶幸的是，這一切反而證明彼此的真愛。另一篇很有名的小說〈重新做人〉，描述一個帥氣十足的撬保險櫃能手，在出獄之後又犯了幾次案，後來他遇到一個美麗的女郎，從此改邪歸正，開了一家鞋店。在快要與這個女郎結婚的時候，她的姪女不小心被關入新金庫中，這時候為了救人，他不顧自己身分曝光的危險（追捕他的警探正守在門外），撬開銀行金庫把孩子救了出來。他想這下子束手就擒吧，沒想到警探大受感動，給予他重生的機會。

在短暫的一生裡，歐亨利作品產量甚豐，出獄後，他隱居紐約，在一九〇四年他就寫了六十四篇，收錄成短篇小說集《捲心菜與國王》（*Cabbages and Kings*），隔年又寫了五十

歐亨利中年以後難得一見的照片。

篇。另一部短篇小說集《四百萬》（*The Four Million*）問世，其中收錄〈聖誕禮物〉。他在世時，共結集成十四部短篇小說集，而在他死後又推出三部短篇小說集。

在美國，根據歐亨利的小說改編的電影至少有一百三十部，電視影集有四十部。他的小說裡沒有色情、暴力、恐怖、邪惡等情節，適合大人小孩閱讀。但有些嚴肅書評家給他的文學評價並不高，說來，這也是文壇的「反諷」，就像日本小說家村上春樹慨嘆自己因書大賣，被日本文壇瞧不起。

今天，美國年年舉辦歐亨利短篇小說獎以紀念他。

The Caledonia
28 4.26

Friday

My dear Mr Davis:

Sick-a-bed until yesterday since Monday. Call if next Monday or Tuesday and I'll have the story with you, or "your money back"

Yours very truly

Sydney Porter

Mr C.B. Davis

歐亨利寫給編輯的親筆函，他簽的是本名。

# 聖誕禮物
# The Gift of the Magi

# New York, 1902

## *CD★ 1*

Narrator：That sound you hear is an elevated train rushing up Sixth Avenue in New York City. The year is 1902. It's a different world. One where a cup of coffee costs a nickel, a postage stamp costs two cents, and that's what you pay for the daily paper—two cents.

Narrator：It's the Christmas season, and there's snow on the ground, lots of it. Can you hear the clopping of horses' hoofs and the creak of wagons? There's hardly an automobile of any sort; they haven't caught on yet. And over there at the corner of 16th Street is Gorman's rooming house. Mrs. Gorman gets eight dollars a week for that dingy little room right on the elevated train tracks. It's rented by Jim and Della Young. They've been married a year, and they're oh-so-in-love.

Narrator：Jim has just come home from his job as a draftsman in an architect's office.

# 紐約，1902

CD★ 1

旁白：你們所聽見的聲音，是一輛急駛在紐約市第六大道上的高架鐵道火車。時間是一九〇二年。那是一個迥然不同的世界，一杯咖啡只要五分錢，一張郵票兩分錢，買份報紙也是一樣——兩分錢。

旁白：這是聖誕季節，地面上積雪很深。你聽到馬蹄躂躂和馬車吱吱嘎嘎行進的聲音嗎？街上幾乎看不到任何汽車，因為那年頭還不流行以車子代步。十六街的轉角是高曼的出租公寓，靠近高架鐵道旁的那個灰暗的小房間，高曼太太每個星期收取八塊錢租金。這房間由吉姆．楊和黛拉．楊夫婦租下，他們倆結婚一年了，而且深深愛著對方。

旁白：吉姆在一家建築師事務所擔任繪圖員，他剛下班回家。

elevated train (*n.*) 高架鐵道火車
nickel (*n.*) 美金五分錢
postage (*n.*) 郵資、郵費
clopping (*n.*) 蹄聲、躂躂聲、得得聲
hoof (*n.*) 蹄
creak (*n.*) 吱吱嘎嘎聲
wagon (*n.*) 四輪馬車
hardly (*adv.*) 幾乎沒有
sort (*n.*) 種、類
catch on 流行（過去式及過去分詞：caught on）
rooming house 有附家具的租賃房子
dingy (*adj.*) 昏暗的
track (*n.*) 軌道
draftsman (*n.*) 繪圖員
architect (*n.*) 建築師

吉姆和黛兒借租在紐約市靠近高架鐵道旁，一個灰暗的小房間。

Del：Seven o'clock again? Oh, you poor darling. You must be dog-tired.

Jim：I am. It's fierce to have to work that hard for twenty dollars a week. But things will get better, honey, don't you worry.

Del：I know they will.

【sound of carolers singing】

dog-tired （*adj.*）
累壞了的
fierce （*adj.*）
極端的、可怕的、非常糟糕的

黛兒：「又拖到七點才回家？哦，可憐的寶貝，你一定累壞了。」

吉姆：「是啊，為了每星期賺個二十塊錢這樣辛苦工作，真慘。不過，別擔心，親愛的，情況會好轉的。」

黛兒：「我也這麼想。」

【聖誕歌聲傳來】

# Day after tomorrow is Christmas

CD★ 2

Del：Oh, listen, Jim, isn't that pretty? Kids across the street singing Christmas carols.

Jim：Let's see, it's Monday, so day after tomorrow is Christmas.

Del：I know.

Jim：Aren't you happy about that?

Del：Not very.

Jim：What's wrong?

Del：Oh, honey, I love you so much, and I want everything in the world for you. Christmas is going to be so skimpy this year. We don't even have a Christmas tree.

Jim：Just can't afford it, honey.

Del：I know.

# 後天就是聖誕節

CD★ 2

黛兒：「哦，吉姆，你聽，好美的歌聲。對街的孩子們正在唱聖誕頌歌。」

吉姆：「我看看，今天是星期一，所以後天就是聖誕節了。」

黛兒：「我知道。」

吉姆：「妳不高興嗎？」

黛兒：「不太高興。」

吉姆：「怎麼啦？」

黛兒：「哦，親愛的，我多麼愛你，我希望把世上的一切都獻給你。今年的聖誕節會過得很寒酸，我們連一棵聖誕樹都沒有。」

吉姆：「我們買不起啊，甜心。」

黛兒：「我知道。」

carol （*n.*） 聖誕頌歌
skimpy （*adj.*） 貧乏的、不足的、簡陋的

一群孩子在葛瑪溪公園玩雪嬉戲。

Jim：I wish I can give you everything you deserve. You're so beautiful. I love everything about you—your eyes, your pretty lips, your beautiful hair.

Del：Huh, huh, you do love my hair, don't you?

Jim：I never saw anything like it.

Del：Oh, Jimmy, give me a kiss.

Jim：We've gotta get out of this place; I can't even kiss my girl in peace and quiet. Listen, let's walk over to Gramercy Park; it's snowing; it'll be fun.

Del：I'd love that.

聖誕鈴聲也響起了。

吉姆：「我多希望我能給妳應得的一切。妳這麼美，我喜歡妳的一切——妳的眼睛，妳那美麗的雙唇，迷人的秀髮。」

黛兒：「哈哈，你真的喜歡我的頭髮，對不對？」

吉姆：「這是我看過最美麗的頭髮。」

黛兒：「哦，吉米，親我一下。」

吉姆：「我們出去吧，我連親我的寶貝都不得安寧。這樣吧，我們走去葛瑪溪公園，外面下著雪，一定很好玩。」

黛兒：「太好了。」

deserve （*v.*） 應得
lip （*n.*） 嘴唇

# The largest topaz

*CD★ 3*

Jim：Isn't the snow dandy? Look how big the flakes are. Won't last long.

Del：Don't say that. We want a *white* Christmas.

Jim：Still a lot of people out shopping. Look at them all over there in front of the jewelry shop. I wonder what's got them hooked.

Del：Maybe they have a monkey in the window?

Jim：Putting the rings on his toes, huh?

Del：Giggles.

Jim：Excuse me, sir, what's the crowd about?

Customer A：Claim they have the largest topaz in the world in the window there. I think it's glass.

Jim：Let's look, honey. Excuse me, sir. Pardon me.

# 最大的黃玉

CD★ 3

吉姆：「好美的雪花。妳看，好大的雪花片片，下不了多久的。」

黛兒：「別這麼說，我們希望有個白色聖誕。」

吉姆：「外頭還是有許多人在逛街購物。那間珠寶店前面擠了好多人，不知道是什麼東西吸引住他們。」

黛兒：「或許是櫥窗裡展示一隻猴子？」

吉姆：「腳趾頭上還戴著戒指，咦？」

黛兒：「哈哈哈。」

吉姆：「抱歉，先生，請問一下那些人在幹嘛?」

顧客甲：「店家宣稱有全世界最大的黃玉，我認為那只是玻璃。」

吉姆：「我們過去看看，甜心。抱歉，先生，借過一下。」

dandy （*adj.*） 漂亮的
flake （*n.*） 雪片
last （*v.*） 持續
in front of 在…前面
jewelry shop 珠寶店
hook （*v.*） 勾住、迷住
ring （*n.*） 戒指
crowd （*n.*） 群衆
claim （*v.*） 宣稱
topaz （*n.*） 黃玉
pardon （*v.*） 原諒

聖誕前夕的購物人潮。

Customer B：Now that would be a real Christmas present.

Customer A：Couldn't wear it. It's too heavy. You'd have to put your hand in a sling.

Jim：Certainly is a big one.

present (*n.*) 禮物
sling (*n.*)
(手受傷時用的)吊帶、吊腕帶

顧客乙：「這才是真正的聖誕禮物。」

顧客甲：「根本不能戴，太重了。你的手得用吊腕帶吊著。」

吉姆：「真的好大喔。」

# Platinum watch fob

*CD★ 4*

Del：Oh, Jimmy, look there — that platinum watch fob.

Jim：Wow, that's beautiful, isn't it? Wouldn't I like to have that.

Del：It would be just right with your granddaddy's watch.

Jim：It sure would. But, honey, quit dreaming. Twenty-one dollars. It says so right there beside it. That's more than a week's pay for me. Come on.

Del：All right.

Jim：Excuse me. Pardon me. Excuse me.

【singing of a Christmas carol】

Del：Listen, there're the kids singing again.

# 白金錶鏈

CD★ 4

platinum （*n.*） 白金
fob （*n.*） 懷錶短鏈
pay （*n.*） 薪水、工資

黛兒：「啊，吉米，你看那邊，那條白金錶鏈。」

吉姆：「哇，好漂亮啊。真希望我能有一副。」

黛兒：「跟你那只古董錶很搭配。」

吉姆：「說的也是。不過，親愛的，別作夢了。二十一塊錢，旁邊有標價。我一周的薪水都買不起，算了吧。」

黛兒：「好吧。」

吉姆：「抱歉，借過一下，抱歉。」

【聖誕歌聲傳來】

黛兒：「你聽，那些孩子又開始唱了。」

Jim：Yeah, someday, Della, I'm gonna make this town sit up and take notice. And you'll have the world's largest topaz, and tortoise shell combs in that beautiful hair; and the combs will be inlaid with diamonds. You wait and see.

Del：I love you, Jimmy, I don't need a topaz. They sing so sweet, that's real Christmas. Listen!

吉姆：「是啊，黛拉，總有一天，我會出人頭地，讓大家刮目相看。妳將擁有全世界最大的黃玉，還有玳瑁髮梳插在妳那美麗的秀髮上，髮梳上面還鑲著鑽石。妳等著看吧。」

黛兒：「我愛你，吉米，我才不要什麼黃玉。他們的歌聲好美，聖誕節就應該是這樣子。你聽！」

sit up （因為感興趣驚訝等而）坐起來
take notice 注意
tortoise shell 玳瑁
comb （*n.*）
梳子（此處為插在頭髮上作裝飾用）
inlay（*v.*） 鑲嵌
（過去式及過去分詞：inlaid）
diamond （*n.*） 鑽石

# A dollar and eighty-seven cents

*CD★ 5*

Narrator：Next morning, when Jimmy had gone to work, Della got down the little jar where she kept the pennies and nickels she'd been so carefully saving ever since their wedding day.

Del：A dollar eighty-one, eighty-two, eighty-three. Oh no, four left. What can I buy him for a dollar eighty-seven cents?

【sound of a knock on the door】

Del：Who is it?

Mabel：It's me, Del.

Del：Oh... hi, Mabel, come on in.

Mabel：I brought you some coffee.

Del：Oh, aren't you nice.

# 一塊八毛七分

jar (*n.*) 罐子
penny (*n.*) 面額小的硬幣
ever since 從…時候起
wedding (*n.*) 結婚

*CD★ 5*

旁白：隔天早晨吉米上班之後，黛拉拿出她用來放銅板的小罐子，這是她從結婚那一天起就省吃儉用存下的零錢。

黛兒：「一塊八毛一、八毛二、八毛三，喔，不妙，只剩四分。一塊八毛七能買什麼給他呢？」

【有人敲門】

黛兒：「哪一位？」

梅波：「黛兒，是我。」

黛兒：「喔……嗨，梅波，請進。」

梅波：「我幫妳帶了一些咖啡。」

黛兒：「喔，妳真好。」

Mabel：What's wrong? You don't look very happy.

Del：I'm not.

Mabel：Well, then what's wrong? You and Jim have a fight or something?

Del：Oh, no, nothing like that. We never fight.

Mabel：But you look like you're about to burst into tears.

Del：Look, look on the table there. A dollar and eighty-seven cents. That's all I've got in the world to buy a Christmas present for Jim. What can I get for a dollar eighty-seven cents, for heaven's sakes?

Mabel：Well, I saw a rocking chair in the furniture store down the street for a dollar and a half.

Del：But I don't want to get him a rocking chair. I'll get him a rocking chair when we're sixty years old or something. Now I wanna get him something he'll treasure all his life.

梅波：「怎麼啦？妳看起來好像不大開心。」

黛兒：「我是不開心。」

梅波：「啊，怎麼搞的？是不是跟吉姆吵架了？」

黛兒：「哦，沒有，沒那回事。我們從來沒吵過架。」

梅波：「可是，妳看起來好像快要哭了。」

黛兒：「看，妳看桌上，只有一塊八毛七分。我只有這些錢替吉姆買聖誕禮物。老天啊，一塊八毛七能買什麼東西呢？」

梅波：「我在家具店看到一張搖椅，只要一塊半。」

黛兒：「可是我根本不想幫他買搖椅。等到我們六十多歲時，我再買吧。現在，我想買給他一個讓他一輩子珍藏的東西。」

fight（*n.*）吵架
burst into
突然發出、迸出
for heaven's sakes
看在老天爺的份上
rocking chair 搖椅
furniture（*n.*）家具
treasure（*v.*）
珍藏、珍視

# Long hair

CD★ 6

Mabel：Like what?

Del：Like that platinum watch fob we saw in Feldstein's Jewelry Store window last night. He fell in love with it.

Mabel：Platinum watch fob! That would set you back some.

Del：Twenty-one dollars. And all I've got in the world is a dollar and eighty-seven cents. I need twenty dollars.

Mabel：You could sell your hair.

Del：Sell my hair? You can't be serious.

Mabel：You can get a lot of money for it. Madam Sofronie down the block...

Del：I won't cut my hair! Jim would kill me. Do you think she'd give twenty dollars for my hair?

Mabel：I don't know. How long is your hair?

# 長髮

CD★ 6

梅波：「比方說呢？」

黛兒：「比方說，我們昨晚在費爾斯坦珠寶店櫥窗看到的那條白金錶鏈，他一看就喜歡。」

梅波：「白金錶鏈！那可要花妳不少錢。」

黛兒：「要二十一塊錢。而我總共只有一塊八毛七，還差二十塊錢。」

梅波：「妳可以賣頭髮。」

黛兒：「賣我的頭髮？妳開什麼玩笑。」

梅波：「妳可以賣給街上索弗朗妮夫人的店，賣很多錢……」

黛兒：「我才不要把頭髮剪掉！吉姆會殺了我。妳想我的頭髮可以賣到二十塊錢嗎？」

梅波：「我不知道。妳的頭髮有多長？」

fall in love with 愛上…
set... back 使…花費
madam (*n.*)（對女士的尊稱）太太、小姐、夫人
block (*n.*) 街區

黛兒有一頭長及膝的漂亮頭髮。

Del：Well, look.

Mabel：Golly, it reaches below your knees!

Del：Jimmy would kill me. How much would she cut off?

Mabel：I don't know. Another girlfriend of mine sold her hair, not to Madam Sofronie, but that one really cut it pretty short. I've gotta be honest with you.

Del：And then what did your friend do? I mean, how did she fix her hair?

golly （*interj.*）哎呀！天哪！
reach （*v.*） 達到
knee （*n.*） 膝蓋
honest （*adj.*）誠實的

黛兒：「嗯，妳瞧！」

梅波：「天哪，一直到妳的膝蓋以下！」

黛兒：「吉米會殺了我。妳想她會剪多長？」

梅波：「我不知道。我一個女朋友賣掉她的頭髮，不是賣給索弗朗妮夫人，但她的頭髮被剪得很短。我得跟妳老實說。」

黛兒：「然後呢？妳那個朋友怎麼整理她的頭髮？」

Mabel：Well, she put it up in curls, you know. And I've got to say, she kinda looked like one of those Coney Island chorus girls.

Del：Oh, Jimmy would kill me. Mabel, do you have a curling iron?

Mabel：Sure, honey. You're getting set to do it, aren't you!

Del：Maybe. Let's go down and talk to that Madam Sofronie.

梅波：「嗯，她把頭髮燙成捲捲的。說真的，她那副模樣有點像康尼島遊樂場裡的賣唱姑娘。」

黛兒：「哦，吉米會殺了我。梅波，妳有沒有燙髮鉗？」

梅波：「當然有啊，親愛的。妳決定這麼做了，是不是？」

黛兒：「有可能。我們去找索弗朗妮夫人談談。」

curl （*n.*） 捲曲的頭髮
Coney Island 康尼島（美國紐約長島上的遊樂場和海水浴場）
chorus （*n.*） 合唱團
curling iron （*n.*） 燙髮鉗（從前用來燙頭髮的鐵鉗）
set （*adj.*） 準備好的

# Jim and Bill

*CD★ 7*

Narrator：Over on the other side of town, in the architect's office where Jim works with his friend Bill, Christmas is also the subject of the conversation.

Bill：If you had the money, Jimmy, what would you get for Del?

亞利桑那州梅薩市摩門教堂的聖誕夜景。（成寒　攝）

# 吉姆與比爾

subject (*n.*) 主題

*CD★ 7*

旁白：城市的另一頭，在吉姆與好友比爾工作的建築師事務所裡，兩人聊的話題也是聖誕節。

比爾：「吉米，假如手上有錢的話，你打算送什麼禮物給黛兒？」

鳳凰城的聖誕夜，居民把自家前院的仙人掌及各種植物掛滿了聖誕燈泡。（成寒　攝）

Jim：I was thinking about a gold bracelet, maybe, Or... or even one of those, you know, pearl necklaces with the cultured pearls, but forget it. After the pay cut we got, it's not in the cards.

Bill：I saw something that's just made for that beautiful hair of Del's.

Jim：What's that?

Bill：In the window downstairs, Mr. Corso's got some tortoise shell combs. They're inlaid with diamonds.

Jim：Don't tell me about it; I saw them. In fact, Della and I even priced them. Do you know how much they are?

Bill：No.

吉姆：「我原本想買副黃金手鐲，或是養珠項鍊。算了吧，我們減薪之後，這些東西想都別想。」

比爾：「我看到一樣東西，正適合黛兒美麗的頭髮。」

吉姆：「什麼東西？」

比爾：「就在樓下，柯索先生的櫥窗裡有一些玳瑁髮梳，上面還鑲了鑽石。」

吉姆：「還用你說，我也看到了。事實上，我跟黛拉還問過價錢，你知道多少錢嗎？」

比爾：「不知道。」

bracelet （*n.*） 手鐲
pearl （*n.*） 珍珠
necklace （*n.*） 項鍊
cultured pearl 養珠
pay cut 減薪
in the cards 可能實現的、可能會發生的
price （*v.*） 問價錢、詢價

# Grandfather's watch

*CD★ 8*

Jim：Twenty-five bucks!

Bill：Ew! That's highway robbery!

Bill：Well, I got to get back to work. What time is it?

Jim：It's exactly 10:30.

# 祖父的錶

CD★ 8

吉姆：「二十五塊。」

比爾：「哇！簡直是攔路搶劫！」

比爾：「唉，我得回去幹活了。幾點啦？」

吉姆：「十點半整。」

buck (*n.*) 一元
highway robbery
攔路搶劫：(1)指從前的強盜埋伏在路邊，伺機搶劫過路商旅；(2)指要價太高，形同搶劫。

Bill：That's what the clock out there says. That old watch of yours keeps darn good time.

Jim：It's been doing it for sixty years. I told you it belonged to my grandfather.

Bill：Solid gold. It's a beauty.

Mr. Potter：You fellas going to spend the whole morning gossiping, like a couple of old ladies over the back fence?

Jim：Oh no, Mr. Potter, we were just talking about Christmas.

Mr. Potter：Well, give me a Christmas present and get back to work.

Bill：Yes, sir.

比爾：「外面的鐘指著十點半，你那只舊錶還走得挺準的。」

吉姆：「六十年來都是這麼準。我告訴過你，這是我爺爺傳下來的。」

比爾：「純金的，好漂亮。」

波特先生：「你們倆想學那些湊在後院籬笆旁的三姑六婆，一整個早上都在說長道短？」

吉姆：「哦，沒有啦，波特先生，我們只是在聊聖誕節的事情。」

波特先生：「好吧，你們可以送個聖誕禮物給我——馬上回去幹活。」

比爾：「遵命，老闆。」

keep good time
（鐘錶）準時
darn （*adv.*）【口語】
非常（＝damned）
belong （*v.*）屬於
gossip （*v.*）
說長道短、閒談
fence （*n.*）籬笆

# Hair Goods, Bought and Sold

*CD★ 9*

Narrator：Back across town, Della and Mabel are standing in the street in front of a shop bearing a sign which reads, "Hair Goods, Bought and Sold－Madam Sofronie."

Mabel：Del, Del! That thing sure makes a peck of noise. Del, this is it. Come on.

Del：I'm half scared to death.

黛兒想賣掉頭髮，換錢買禮物給吉姆。

# 買賣頭髮商品

## CD★ 9

旁白：回到城的這一邊，黛拉和梅波站在街上一家店鋪前，招牌上寫著：「買賣頭髮用品——索弗朗妮夫人。」

梅波：「黛兒，黛兒！那聲音實在是太吵了。黛兒，就是這兒，進來吧。」

黛兒：「我好害怕。」

街角一景。

sign (*n.*) 招牌
goods (*n.*)
商品、物品（用複數形）
sure (*adv.*)
的確、確實
a peck of 許多、大量
noise (*n.*)
喧嘩聲、嘈雜聲
scare (*v.*)
使恐懼、驚嚇

Mabel：Well, you don't have to do it, you know. We'll just ask her how much she'd give you for your hair, and if you decide you don't want to do it, you can always leave.

Del：All right, let's go in.

Mabel：Hello? She must be in the back. Hello? Is there anyone here?

Madam Sofronie：I'm comin'. I'll be there right away.

Mabel：Let your hair down, Del, so she can see what she's buying.

Del：All right. That's it.

梅波：「啊，妳不一定要賣髮，我們只是問問她願意出多少錢。如果妳不想賣，隨時可以走人。」

黛兒：「好吧，我們進去吧。」

梅波：「哈囉？她一定是在後面。哈囉？有人在嗎？」

索弗朗妮夫人：「我來了，我馬上過來。」

梅波：「黛兒，把頭髮放下來，讓她看清楚一點。」

黛兒：「好吧，就是這樣子。」

# A fine-looking head of hair

## CD★10

Mabel：Oh, it's beautiful!

Madam Sofronie：Oh, dearies, oh my, isn't that a fine-looking head of hair.

Mabel：Madam Sofronie, Della here wants to know how much you'll pay her for her hair.

Del：But cut it off just below the shoulders.

Madam Sofronie：Hmm... that's two and a half feet or so... Twelve dollars.

Del：Twelve? That's all?

Mabel：Aw, come on, Madam Sofronie, you can do better than that. If you cut it off close, what would you give her?

Madam Sofronie：Umm... I tell you what I'll do with ya... Sixteen dollars.

# 一頭漂亮的秀髮

shoulder （*n.*） 肩膀
or so 左右、大約

## CD★10

梅波：「噢，好美啊！」

索弗朗妮夫人：「哦，我的小姐啊，天哪，妳有一頭漂亮的秀髮。」

梅波：「索弗朗妮夫人，黛拉想知道妳願意出多少錢買她的頭髮。」

黛兒：「可是，只能剪到肩膀以下。」

索弗朗妮夫人：「嗯……這樣大約有兩呎半……十二塊錢。」

黛兒：「十二塊？才這樣而已？」

梅波：「哦，拜託，索弗朗妮夫人，妳應該可以出更高一點。如果剪得更短一點，妳願意付多少？」

索弗朗妮夫人：「嗯……我看看我可以……十六塊。」

# Irish temper

*CD★11*

Del：No, no, I won't do it for less than twenty dollars. I need twenty dollars. Thank you very much, Madam Sofronie.

Madam Sofronie：Aw, now, wait girl, wait... wait, faith and Begorrah, she's got an Irish temper. You're as Irish as I am.

Mabel：Irish? I thought 'Sofronie' would be Italian or something.

Madam Sofronie：Ha, ha, I'm as Irish as Paddy's pig. My born name's O'Callahan. Sofronie was my husband. It has the right sound for the hair business. Kinda chic, don't you think?

Mabel：Oh, yes, it surely is.

# 愛爾蘭脾氣

CD★11

黛兒：「不行，不行，二十塊以下我死也不肯。我需要二十塊錢。謝謝妳，索弗朗妮夫人。」

索弗朗妮夫人：「噢，等等，小姐，等等，等一下……天啊！她有愛爾蘭人的拗脾氣。妳跟我這個愛爾蘭人很像。」

梅波：「愛爾蘭人？我以為『索弗朗妮』是義大利人的名字呢。」

索弗朗妮夫人：「哈哈，我是如假包換的愛爾蘭人……我本姓歐凱拉罕，索弗朗妮是我先生的姓，聽起來有點時髦，很適合美髮業，不是嗎？」

梅波：「哦，是啊，一點也沒錯。」

faith and Begorrah
【愛爾蘭語】天啊！
temper （*n.*）
易發怒的脾氣
...or something
…之類的
Paddy （*n.*）【俚語】
愛爾蘭（裔）人
chic （*adj.*）
時髦的、漂亮的

Del：I have to have twenty dollars. Come on, Mabel, and thank you very much, Madam Sofronie, for your time.

Madam Sofronie：Oh, it's a stubborn one. It bein' the Christmas season and all...twenty dollars it is. But I want you to understand I'll be cuttin' it pretty close.

Del：You'll give me twenty dollars?

Madam Sofronie：That's what I said, girl. A Christmas present from me to you.

黛兒：「我一定要弄到二十塊錢。梅波，我們走吧。非常感謝妳，索弗朗妮夫人，耽誤妳的時間。」

索弗朗妮夫人：「噢，真是倔強。嗯，既然是聖誕季節…那就算二十塊吧。但我得先讓妳知道，我會剪得很短。」

stubborn (*adj.*)
頑固的、倔強的

黛兒：「妳願意付我二十塊？」

索弗朗妮夫人：「我說過了，小姐，就算是我送給妳的聖誕禮物。」

# Here we go!

CD★12

Del：All right.

Madam Sofronie：Well, let's get on with it. Here, here, sit right down here in this chair. I'll get me scissors. It'll only take a minute, girl. I'll have it off in no time at all.

Del：Oh, Mabel, I'm going to cry.

Mabel：Listen, Del, you're getting twenty dollars. That's what you want, and that's what you need to buy the present for Jim, so don't lose your nerve.

Del：All right, I won't.

Madam Sofronie：Now then, you can look in the mirror or not as you like.

Del：I don't wanna see it. Yes, yes, I do. I don't know.

Mabel：Might as well look. You're gonna have to face up to it sometime.

# 開始剪囉！

CD★12

scissors (*n.*) 剪刀
nerve (*n.*) 勇氣
mirror (*n.*) 鏡子
face up to 勇敢地面對

黛兒：「好吧。」

索弗朗妮夫人：「好吧，我們開始剪囉。來，過來這裡，坐在這張椅子上。我去拿剪刀，一下子，馬上就過來。」

黛兒：「啊，梅波，我好想哭哦。」

梅波：「聽著，黛兒，妳會拿到二十塊錢。那是妳想要的，妳需要那筆錢替吉姆買禮物，勇敢一點。」

黛兒：「好吧，我不哭就是了。」

索弗朗妮夫人：「現在，妳要不要照一下鏡子？」

黛兒：「我不想照。好，好吧，我照一下。我也不知道。」

梅波：「最好還是照一下，反正妳遲早都要面對它。」

索弗朗妮夫人開始剪黛兒的頭髮。

Madam Sofronie：Here we go!

【sound of hair being cut】

Del：Oh, oh...

【sound of hair being cut】

Madam Sofronie：Oh, you're goin' to look so cute, girl. Your hubby will say he never saw the like.

Del：My hubby will kill me, and I won't blame him.

cute（*adj.*）可愛的
hubby（*n.*）【口語】丈夫
blame（*v.*）責怪

索弗朗妮夫人：「開始剪囉。」

【剪頭髮的聲音】

黛兒：「噢，噢……」

【剪頭髮的聲音】

索弗朗妮夫人：「哦，小姐，妳看起來會很可愛，妳老公一定沒看過妳這個樣子。」

黛兒：「我老公會殺了我，可是我不怪他。」

# A skinned rabbit

*CD★13*

【sound of hair being cut】

Madam Sofronie：There, you see how quick it is; I'm half done already.

【sound of hair being cut】

Mabel：Oh, my goodness!

Del：Oh, oh...

Madam Sofronie：Oh, faith and Begorrah, it's a fine head of hair. A fine head of hair. Now it's almost done.

【sound of hair being cut】

Mabel：I think it's going to look all right, Del.

Del：I think it looks terrible.

# 一隻剝了皮的兔子

CD★13

【剪頭髮的聲音】

索弗朗妮夫人：「妳看，很快吧，我已經剪好一半了。」

【剪頭髮的聲音】

梅波：「哦，我的天啊。」

黛兒：「哦，哦……」

索弗朗妮夫人：「噢，天啊，一頭好美的秀髮，真是漂亮。快剪好了。」

【剪頭髮的聲音】

梅波：「黛兒，我覺得妳的樣子看來還好。」

黛兒：「我覺得好醜噢。」

剛剪了頭髮的黛兒覺得自己像一隻剝了皮的兔子。

Madam Sofronie：There we are. Oh, there must be two pounds of it here. Your head's going to feel a whole lot lighter, girl.

Del：I can't believe it. Mabel, let's get out of here.

Mabel：Let's get the twenty dollars first.

Madam Sofronie：Now there's a girl with a head on her shoulders. I'll get it for you right away. It's in the backroom.

pound (*n.*) 磅

索弗朗妮夫人：「好了。嗯，這一定有兩磅重，妳的腦袋會感覺輕鬆多了。」

黛兒：「我真不敢相信。梅波，我們走吧。」

梅波：「二十塊錢還沒拿呢。」

索弗朗妮夫人：「這個女孩總算有頭腦。我馬上拿來給妳，錢放在後面的房間。」

Del：Oh, Mabel, look at me. Look at me! I look like a skinned rabbit. Jim will hate me, just hate me. I hate myself. He loves my hair so.

Mabel：Don't worry, Del. Don't worry. He'll get used to it. He didn't marry you for your hair, you know.

Madam Sofronie：And here it is. A bright, shiny twenty-dollar gold piece. Pretty, ain't it?

Del：Thank you. Thank you, Madame Sofronie.

Mabel：Come on, Del.

Madam Sofronie：Goodbye, girl. Good luck.

Del：Yes, I'll need all the luck I can get.

黛兒：「哦，梅波，妳看，妳看看我這個模樣，像一隻剝了皮的兔子。吉姆一定會討厭我的，一定會的。我討厭我自己，他這麼喜歡我的頭髮。」

梅波：「別擔心，黛兒，別擔心。他很快就會習慣的。他又不是為了妳的頭髮才娶妳。」

索弗朗妮夫人：「這是妳的錢，一枚閃亮的二十元金幣，漂亮吧？」

黛兒：「謝謝妳。謝謝妳，索弗朗妮夫人。」

梅波：「黛兒，我們走吧。」

索弗朗妮夫人：「再見囉，祝妳們好運。」

黛兒：「是啊，我真的需要好運。」

skinned （*adj.*） 剝了皮的

shiny （*adj.*） 發光的

# Little curls

## CD★14

Narrator：The damage was done. Del and Mabel hurried home through the snow to see if there was any way to conceal, repair or improve the carnage wrought by Madame Sofronie's busy scissors.

Mabel：Del, we need to light the gas on the stove so we can heat the curling iron.

Del：He'll kill me. He'll kill me, I tell you, and I won't blame him. Oh, Mabel, look how I look. Isn't that the worst?

Mabel：Oh, come on, Della. It's not as though you lost an arm or a leg or something. It's just hair, and it'll grow back again. So it will take a little time. So what?

Del：So, meantime he'll fall in love with somebody with beautiful long hair like I used to have－that's so what.

# 小髮捲

## CD★14

旁白：損害已經造成。黛兒和梅波冒著大雪趕回家，看看有沒有辦法隱藏、修復、或改善索弗朗妮夫人的利剪所造成的慘劇。

梅波：「黛兒，我們要把爐火打開，把燙髮鉗加熱。」

黛兒：「他會殺了我，他會殺了我！我跟妳說真的，我不會怪他。哦，梅波，妳看我這個模樣，是不是很糟？」

梅波：「哦，算了吧，黛拉。這又不是缺手斷腿什麼的，只是把頭髮剪掉，以後還會再長回來。只是要花點時間，這有什麼關係？」

黛兒：「那麼，這段時間他會愛上別的女孩，因為她有我過去那樣漂亮的長髮——就是這麼一回事。」

damage （*n.*）
損害、損傷
conceal （*v.*） 隱藏
repair （*v.*）
修補、修繕
improve （*v.*）
改善、改進
carnage （*n.*） 大屠殺
wrought （work的過去式及過去分詞，為比較古老的用法）製造
gas （*n.*） 瓦斯
stove （*n.*） 爐子
as though 彷彿、像似

Mabel：Look, honey, just put your mind on that platinum watch fob you're going to buy Jim. Just remember, you got a twenty-dollar gold piece to buy it with.

Del：I know. You're right.

Mabel：Now, let's get to work on your hair. We're going to make it all little curls, all over your head. Jim will love it.

Del：No, he won't.

梅波：「聽我說，親愛的，妳現在只要想著妳要替吉姆買的那條白金錶鏈。只要記住，妳已經有二十塊錢可以買下它。」

黛兒：「我知道，妳說的對。」

梅波：「現在呢，我們去打理妳的頭髮。我們把整個頭髮燙成小捲，吉姆會喜歡的。」

黛兒：「不會，他不會喜歡的。」

# Mr. Feldstein, the jeweler

## CD★15

Narrator：But finally the job was done, and any fair-minded person would have to agree that Della looked as cute as a buck's ear. Her head was all-over curls. She did look a little boyish. And in the fashions of the time, that was somewhat out of place, but she tried to ignore the long stares as she and Mabel hurried across the street late in the afternoon to Mr. Feldstein, the jeweler, where the precious platinum watch fob lay.

Del：It's almost five o'clock. I hope he's still open. I hope he hasn't sold it. Oh, if he sold it...

Mabel：Will you stop that? You're getting *me* nervous. Of course he hasn't sold it. Here we are. Let's get through the crowd here.

Del：Pardon me, please. May I get through here, please? Pardon me, I want to get into the store.

Mabel：Excuse me. Oh, I'm sorry, madam.

# 珠寶商費爾斯坦

CD★15

旁白：終於，燙髮這件事完成了。相信每個正常的人都會同意，黛兒看起來很可愛。現在她滿頭捲髮，有點像小男生，以當時流行趨勢來看，的確有點突兀。那天傍晚，她和梅波急著穿過街道趕往費爾斯坦珠寶店──賣那條白金錶鏈的地方，一路上，她試著不去理會路人的注目眼光。

黛兒：「快五點了，希望他的店還開著，希望他還沒把錶鏈賣掉。噢，萬一他賣掉了…」

梅波：「拜託妳，不要這樣，妳讓我好緊張。他當然還沒賣掉。到了，我們得穿過人群。」

黛兒：「抱歉，借過，請讓我過一下好嗎？抱歉，我要到店裡去。」

梅波：「抱歉，哦，對不起，夫人。」

fair-minded （*adj.*）心智正常的
cute as a bug's ear 很可愛
boyish （*adj.*）男孩似的
out of place 不適合的
ignore （*v.*）忽略、忽視
stare （*n.*）盯、凝視
jeweler （*n.*）珠寶商
precious （*adj.*）寶貴的、貴重的

# It's gone!

CD★16

Del：Mabel!

Mabel：What?

Del：It's gone! It was right there beside the topaz!

Mabel：Oh, no!

Del：And I cut off my hair.

Mabel：Well, let's find out about it. Excuse me, sir. Pardon us, please.

Mr. Feldstein：Good afternoon, I will be with you in a moment.

Del：Mr. Feldstein? Are you Mr. Feldstein...

Mr. Feldstein：Yes.

Del：The platinum watch fob...

# 它不見了！

moment (*n.*)
瞬間、片刻

## CD★16

黛兒：「梅波！」

梅波：「怎樣啦？」

黛兒：「它不見了！它本來放在黃玉旁邊的！」

梅波：「噢，完了。」

黛兒：「而我的頭髮已經剪掉了。」

梅波：「啊，我們去問問看。抱歉，先生，對不起，請問一下。」

費爾斯坦先生：「午安，我一會兒就過來。」

黛兒：「費爾斯坦先生，請問你是費爾斯坦先生嗎？」

費爾斯坦先生：「是的。」

黛兒：「那條白金錶鏈呢？」

Mr. Feldstein：I'll be with you in a moment, young lady. I have a customer.

Del：The platinum watch fob — did you sell it?

Mr. Feldstein：Henry? Henry, will you come here a minute, please? Henry will take care of you. I have a customer.

Henry：Yes, ladies... Yes, ladies, may I help you?

Del：The platinum watch fob—the one that was in the window next to the topaz — it's not there.

Henry：I think it was sold.

Del：Oh, no!

Mabel：Oh, Del.

Henry：Let me go and see.

費爾斯坦先生：「兩位年輕小姐，我馬上過來招呼妳們，我現在有客人。」

黛兒：「那條白金錶鏈，你賣掉了嗎？」

費爾斯坦先生：「亨利，亨利，你過來一下好嗎？讓亨利來招呼妳，我這裡有客人。」

亨利：「是的，兩位小姐，有什麼需要我服務的嗎？」

黛兒：「那條白金錶鏈，原本放在櫥窗裡黃玉旁邊的，不見了。」

亨利：「我想是賣掉了。」

黛兒：「噢，完了。」

梅波：「啊，黛兒。」

亨利：「我去看看。」

customer （*n.*） 顧客

# A deposit

*CD★17*

Del：If... if it's sold... if it's sold... if it's sold, Mabel, what am I gonna do? What am I gonna say to Jim?

Mabel：I don't know. Oh, honey, maybe we can find something somewhere else.

Del：No, this is what he wanted. He saw it in the window last night and...

Henry：I'm sorry, miss, the customer left a deposit on the watch fob at noon today, and he said that he would be by by five o'clock to pick it up. But the watch fob is sold.

Del：Oh!

Henry：Is she going to faint?

Mabel：No, she's not gonna faint. Here, sit down, Della. Sit down in this chair. If he doesn't come back by five o'clock, then what?

# 訂金

deposit (*n.*) 訂金
pick... up 領取
faint (*v.*)
昏厥、昏過去

## CD★17

黛兒：「萬一……萬一賣掉了……萬一賣掉了……萬一真的賣掉了，梅波，我該怎麼辦？我要怎麼跟吉姆交代？」

梅波：「我也不知道。哦，甜心，我們也許可以到別的地方買其他東西。」

黛兒：「不要，這是他想要的東西，他昨晚在櫥窗裡看到就……」

亨利：「小姐，我很抱歉，今天中午有位客人付了訂金買那條錶鏈，他說五點鐘以前會過來拿。」

黛兒：「噢……」

亨利：「她不會昏倒吧？」

梅波：「不會，她不會昏倒。黛拉，這裡有張椅子，妳先坐下。如果他沒在五點以前過來，你們打算怎麼辦呢？」

聖誕夜在聖塔菲，泥磚屋頂邊緣及矮圍牆上擱置一盞又一盞沙袋燈，美如幻夢。（成寒　攝）

Henry：Well, madam, if he doesn't get here by five o'clock we'll simply sell the watch fob to someone else.

Mabel：Wait! She has the money. It's twenty-one dollars, isn't it?

Henry：Yes, that is right.

Mabel：Well, she has the money. She has the money right there in her purse. And if he isn't here by five o'clock, at one second after five, we want that watch fob.

聖塔菲著名的羅瑞托旅店（Inn At Loretto Santa Fe），幾何方塊造形，在聖誕夜點起了沙袋燈，如夢似幻。（成寒　攝）

simply（*adv.*）
僅僅、只
purse（*n.*）
錢包、手提包

亨利：「這個嘛，小姐如果他五點鐘以前沒過來，我們只……只好把錶鏈賣給別人。」

梅波：「我們……她身上有錢，二十一塊錢，沒錯吧？」

亨利：「是的，沒錯。」

梅波：「她有錢，錢就在她的錢包裡頭，如果他五點鐘沒過來，五點過一秒，錶鏈就賣給我們。」

# The minutes ticked by

*CD★18*

Narrator：The minutes ticked by. Della and Mabel kept their eyes fastened on the front door to the store. Every time a man walked in, the girls' hearts sank. But, no one asked for the watch fob.

Mabel：It's five o'clock. Your own clock up there on the wall is saying it. It's five o'clock! Hear that?

【chimes stop】

Henry：When the chimes stop, it is five o'clock.

Mabel：It's five o'clock.

Del：It's five o'clock. Here's the money— twenty-one dollars.

Henry：Yes, a gold piece and four quarters. Mr. Feldstein? Mr. Feldstein?

# 時間一分一秒過去

CD★18

旁白：時間一分一秒過去，黛拉和梅波目不轉睛盯著店舖前。每當有人走進來，她們的心便一沉。不過，沒有一個人來取錶鏈。

梅波：「五點了。你們牆上的鐘正好五點。五點，聽到了嗎？」

【鐘聲停止】

亨利：「鐘聲一停止，就是五點整。」

梅波：「五點鐘了。」

黛兒：「五點了。錢在這兒，二十一塊。」

亨利：「沒錯，一枚二十塊金幣和四枚兩毛五。費爾斯坦先生，費爾斯坦先生。」

tick （*v.*） 滴答滴答響
fasten （*v.*） 鎖緊、拴牢、盯住
chime （*n.*） 鐘聲

# Five o'clock

CD★19

Mr. Feldstein：Yes, yes, what...what is it, Henry?

Henry：These ladies want to purchase the platinum watch fob—the one there's a deposit on. The customer said he would be by to pick it up at five o'clock. It's now five, and he's not here, and these ladies have given me the money for the watch fob.

Mr. Feldstein：Well, I... I don't know. I think we ought to give the customer who put down the deposit... uh... a moment or two of grace.

Del：Mr. Feldstein, I had my hair cut off and sold it to buy that platinum watch fob for my husband for Christmas.

Mr. Feldstein：My gracious, you did have it cut off! Isn't that interesting?

Henry：Very interesting.

# 五點鐘

CD★19

費爾斯坦先生：「來了，來了，什麼事，亨利？」

亨利：「這兩位小姐想買那條白金錶鏈，但已經有人付了訂金。那位客人說他五點之前會來取貨。現在已經五點了，他人還沒到，這兩位小姐想付錢買下這條錶鏈。」

費爾斯坦先生：「嗯，我……我不知道，我想應該給那位付訂金的客人多一點時間……嗯……等會兒再說吧。」

黛兒：「費爾斯坦先生，我把剪掉頭髮賣的錢來替我老公買那條錶鏈，作為聖誕禮物。」

費爾斯坦先生：「天哪，妳真的把頭髮剪了！真有意思！」

亨利：「真的很有意思。」

purchase （*v.*） 購買
ought to 應該
grace （*n.*） 寬限
gracious （*adj.*）
優雅的、仁慈的（作感嘆詞使用時是「天啊！」之意）
my gracious
我的老天！

Mabel：Do we get the watch fob, or don't we?

Del：Please, Mr. Feldstein.

Mr. Feldstein：Wrap up the watch fob, Henry, and make a pretty package of it for this pretty young lady.

Del：You think I'm pretty? Oh, that's the nicest thing you ever said, Mr. Feldstein, that you think I'm pretty.

Mr. Feldstein：Pretty as a picture, and I hope your husband enjoys the watch fob and appreciates it. I hope it looks wonderful on his watch. Merry Christmas to you. What a noble thing to do for her husband. I wish to him... well, never mind. Merry Christmas, young ladies. Henry, wrap the gift for them.

Del：Oh, thank you, Mr. Feldstein. Thank you!

梅波：「錶鏈到底要不要賣給我們？」

黛兒：「費爾斯坦先生，拜託你。」

費爾斯坦先生：「亨利，把錶鏈包起來，替這位漂亮小姐包得漂漂亮亮的。」

黛兒：「你覺得我漂亮嗎？哦，你說我漂亮，那是你對我說過最動聽的話，費爾斯坦先生。」

費爾斯坦先生：「像畫一樣漂亮，但願妳老公喜歡這錶鏈，也能體會妳的心意。希望和他的錶能夠搭配。祝妳聖誕快樂。她對老公真好。我希望他……嗯……沒什麼。兩位小姐聖誕快樂。亨利，替她們把禮物包起來。」

黛兒：「哦，謝謝你，費爾斯坦先生，謝謝你。」

wrap up 包裝
package （*n.*） 包裹
appreciate （*v.*） 體會，感激
noble （*adj.*） 崇高的

一群唱詩班小孩。

聖誕夜在聖塔菲，居民在門前及屋簷上擺滿了沙袋燈。（成寒　攝）

# Gift wrapping

*CD★20*

Narrator：Henry brought back the watch fob, wrapped in the most beautiful paper Mr. Feldstein could provide. Now Della was radiant and full to bursting with the Christmas spirit. As they crossed Sixth Avenue, the girls heard the carolers who had been there the night before.

【sound of carolers】

Del：Listen, Mabel, it's the kids again. Jim probably won't be home till seven o'clock. Let's stop and listen a minute.

【sound of carolers singing a couple of songs】

# 包裝禮物

## CD★20

旁白：亨利取回那條錶鏈，用費爾斯坦先生店裡最美麗的包裝紙包起來。此刻，黛拉神采奕奕，滿懷聖誕節的情緒。當她們穿過第六大道時，又聽到昨晚那群唱詩班的歌聲。

【唱詩班的歌聲傳來】

黛兒：「梅波，妳聽，又是那些孩子們。吉姆大概七點鐘以前還不會回家，我們停下來聽一會兒。」

【唱詩班唱了幾首歌曲】

provide (*v.*) 提供
radiant (*adj.*)
發光的、燦爛的、容光煥發的
spirit (*n.*)
精神、氣氛
caroler (*n.*)
唱詩班的一員、唱頌歌的人

# Broke

*CD★21*

Del：That's so pretty! Well, I'd better be getting home. I wanna get things tidied up before I have to face Jimmy with my boy's haircut. But, I feel so much better now, now that I have his present right here in my hand.

Mabel：Any idea what he's going to give you?

Del：I don't know, and I don't care. It's what I give him that counts with me. I suppose it'll be something simple: a box of candy or something, because he's just as broke as I am, and he doesn't have any hair to sell.

Mabel：That's the first laugh I've heard out of you today.

Del：I know, but I'm still scared.

Mabel：Della, just remember, Jimmy loves you. You got nothing to worry about.

Del：I hope so.

# 一文不名

CD★21

黛兒：「歌聲真美！唉，我最好趕快回去。我要在吉米看到我的男孩模樣之前，把家裡整理收拾好。不過，我現在覺得好多了，至少手上拿著要送給他的禮物。」

梅波：「妳猜他會送妳什麼？」

黛兒：「我不知道，反正我無所謂。我只在乎我能給他什麼東西。我想應該是很簡單的東西，一盒糖果或什麼的，因為他跟我一樣口袋空空，而且他也沒有頭髮可以拿去賣，哈哈哈。」

梅波：「我今天還頭一回聽妳笑。」

黛兒：「我知道，但我還是很害怕。」

梅波：「黛拉，妳只要記得，吉米很愛妳，沒什麼好擔心的。」

黛兒：「但願如此。」

tidy up　收拾、整理（過去式及過去分詞：tidied up）
haircut （*n.*） 理髮
count （*v.*） 重要
broke （*adj.*）
身無分文的、破產的

# Footsteps

## CD★22

Narrator：Della dropped Mabel at the door, then she primped and tidied up the drab little room as best she could and waited for the man she loved. Promptly at seven, she heard those familiar footsteps on the stairs. She took a deep breath, posed herself on the corner of the table and waited.

Jim：I'm home, honey.

Del：Hello, Jimmy.

Jim：You're usually at the...

Del：Jim, Jim? Say something, Jim. Jim, darling, don't look at me that way. I had my hair cut off and sold it because I couldn't have lived through Christmas without giving you a present. It'll grow out again－you won't mind, will you? I just had to do it. My hair grows awful fast. Say 'Merry Christmas!' Jim. Let's be happy. You don't know what a beautiful, nice gift I have for you.

# 腳步聲

## CD★22

旁白：黛拉在門口和梅波道別，然後把簡陋的小房間整理收拾好，等待她所愛的男人回來。七點鐘一到，她就聽見樓梯響起熟悉的腳步聲。她深深吸了一口氣，在桌子的角落靜候等待。

吉姆：「甜心，我回來了。」

黛兒：「嗨，吉米。」

吉姆：「妳平常都會在……」

黛兒：「吉姆……吉姆……說話嘛，吉姆……吉姆，親愛的，別那樣盯著我。我把頭髮剪掉賣了，因為不送你一件禮物，我過不了聖誕節。頭髮會再長回來的──你不會在意吧？我非這麼做不可。我的頭髮長得很快。說句『聖誕快樂』吧！吉姆，讓我們快快樂樂的。你不知道我給你買了一件多麼好、多麼美麗的禮物。」

primp （*v.*） 整理
drab （*adj.*） 單調的、乏味的
promptly （*adv.*） 準時地
footstep （*n.*） 腳步聲
stairs （*n.*） 樓梯
breath （*n.*） 呼吸
pose （*v.*） 擺姿勢

吉姆一走進門，看到黛兒在桌子的角落靜候等待。

Jim：You cut off your hair!

Del：Don't you like me just as much anyhow? I'm me even without my hair. Jim.

Jim：Oh, honey darling.

吉姆：「妳把頭髮剪掉了？」

黛兒：「不管怎樣，你還是同樣喜歡我吧？雖然沒有了頭髮，我還是我啊！吉姆。」

吉姆：「哦，我親愛的寶貝。」

# Unwrapping the gift

## *CD★23*

Del：Oh, I feel so good in your arms.

Jim：Don't make any mistake about me, gal... I don't think there's anything in the way of a haircut that can make me like my gal less. Here, here's something I bought you. Let me get it out of my pocket here. If you'll unwrap that package, you may see why you had me going there at first.

Del：What is it? I can't wait to see what it is. It certainly is expensive paper, and beautifully wrapped. The combs! The combs for my hair, the ones we saw in the window. You bought them. Oh, darling, I love you so much. They're so wonderful! How did you ever afford them, Jim? How...oh, I forgot. I completely forgot. I have a present for you. That's why I sold my hair. Here, here it is. Now, you open it.

【sound of a box being unwrapped】

# 打開包裝盒

*CD★23*

黛兒：「噢，在你懷裡的感覺真好。」

吉姆：「不要誤會我，小姑娘…不管妳的頭髮剪成怎樣，我對我姑娘的愛不會減少半分。這是我買給妳的東西，在我的口袋裡。妳打開那包東西就會明白，為什麼剛才妳讓我愣住了。」

黛兒：「什麼東西啊？我等不及了。這種包裝紙很貴，包得很漂亮。是髮梳！可以梳我的頭髮，就是我們在櫥窗裡看到的那支。你居然買了下來。噢，親愛的，我好愛你。好美的髮梳！吉姆，你怎麼買得起呢？哦，我忘了，我完全忘了，我也有禮物要給你，那就是為什麼我去把頭髮賣掉的原因。在這裡，打開看看。」

【拆開包裝盒的聲音】

gal （*n.*）
女孩子、少女
pocket （*n.*） 口袋
unwrap （*v.*）
打開包裝
at first 最初
expensive （*adj.*）
高價的
afford （*v.*）
買得起、負擔得起

Del：Now, open the box! Open the box!

吉姆買下玳瑁梳子送給黛兒，作為聖誕禮物。

黛兒：「現在，把盒子打開！打開啊！」

黛兒送給吉姆的禮物是白金錶鏈。

# Christmas presents

*CD★24*

Jim：Della, the watch fob!

Del：Isn't it beautiful? Remember we saw it in the jeweler's window last night?

Jim：That's what you sold your hair for.

Del：Isn't it beautiful, Jim? You'll have to look at the time a hundred times a day now. Give me your watch. I wanna see what it looks like with it.

Jim：Del, let's put our Christmas presents away and keep 'em a while. They're too nice to use at present.

Del：Don't you like it, Jim? Don't you want it?

Jim：Del, I...I sold my watch to buy you the combs.

# 聖誕禮物

## CD★24

吉姆：「黛拉，是那條錶鏈！」

黛兒：「好看嗎？你想起來了沒？這是我們昨晚在珠寶店櫥窗裡看到的那條。」

吉姆：「妳就是為了這個去賣掉頭髮？」

黛兒：「吉姆，你覺得好看嗎？現在你每天要把錶看上百來遍。把你的錶給我，我想看看它配在錶上的樣子。」

吉姆：「黛拉，我們把聖誕禮物擱在一邊，暫且收起來。它們實在太好啦，現在用了未免太可惜。」

黛兒：「你不喜歡嗎？吉姆，你不想要嗎？」

吉姆：「黛拉，我……我賣掉了錶，換了錢去買妳的髮梳。」

兩人深深相愛，這是人間最美好的聖誕節。

# The Magi

CD★25

Narrator：The magi, as you know, were wise men—wonderfully wise men who brought gifts to the babe in the manger. But in a last word to the wise these days, let it be said that of all those who give gifts, these two young lovers were the wisest. As Jim and Della clung to one another, out in the snowy street below, the carolers' voices rose to greet Christmas, and nowhere was the spirit of Christmas more real than in that little room overlooking the elevated train in New York town. Quietly, the young lovers listened.

【sound of carolers】

Del：Merry Christmas, Jim, and it's the very best Christmas anyone could ever have.

【sound of carolers】

# 東方三賢士

CD★25

旁白：那東方三賢士，諸位知道，全是有智慧的人——非常有智慧的人——他們帶來禮物，送給生在馬槽裡的耶穌。但是，讓我們對今天所有的聰明人說最後一句話：在所有饋贈禮物的人當中，這兩個年輕戀人是最聰明的。吉姆和黛拉緊緊依偎彼此，外頭積雪的街道上，唱詩班唱起了頌歌，迎接聖誕節的到來。沒有一個地方比這個俯視紐約市高架鐵道的小房間裡更富有聖誕氣氛。這對年輕戀人靜靜地傾聽。

magi 請參考書後解說
babe （*n.*） 嬰孩
manger （*n.*） 馬槽
cling （*v.*）
緊緊依偎（過去式及過去分詞：clung）
rise （*v.*）
提高、揚起（過去式及過去分詞：rose, risen）
greet （*v.*）
迎接、問候、致敬
overlook （*v.*） 俯瞰

【唱詩班的歌聲傳來】

黛兒：「聖誕快樂，吉姆，這真是人間最美好的聖誕節。」

【唱詩班的歌聲傳來】

Narrator：Gift of the Magi, one of the world's best stories, was written by William Sidney Porter, better known as O. Henry. Thank you for spending a little bit of Christmas with us.

旁白：〈聖誕禮物〉，這個家喻戶曉的故事，作者是威廉·席尼·波特，他有個大家更熟知的筆名——歐亨利。謝謝你們和我們一起度過聖誕節的一小段時光。

東方三賢士。

# 東方三賢士

Magi 這個字源出聖經《新約》馬太福音二章，可譯作「東方三賢士」，也就是耶穌誕生後，從東方前來朝拜耶穌獻上禮物的三位賢士，或譯「智者」（wise men）或「三個國王」。

三王的名字分別是加斯帕（Casper，清白者）、梅爾基奧爾（Melchior，光明之王）和巴爾撒澤（Balthasar）。當耶穌降世時，三王根據天上一顆星的指引，從東方來到耶路撒冷旁的小城伯利恆（Bethlehem）——耶穌誕生的地方，和牧童們一起朝拜，並獻上所帶的禮物。加斯帕獻上「乳香」（incense），象徵神聖；梅爾基奧爾獻上黃金，象徵尊貴；巴爾撒澤獻上「沒藥」（myrrh），象徵永生。

在基督教傳說中，Magi 首創了世人今天聖誕節饋贈禮物的習俗。耶穌降生於12月24日子夜，亦即25日零時，是以西方傳統習俗，慶祝聖誕節是從12月24日晚開始，稱為「聖誕前夕」或「聖誕夜」（Christmas Eve）。東方三賢士是在元月6日見到聖嬰，是日即為主顯節（Epiphany）。

# 與聖誕節有關的英文語彙

green Christmas　沒有雪的聖誕節

white Christmas　有雪的聖誕節

Christmastime或Christmastide　聖誕節節期：12月24日至元月6日主顯節

Christmassy　有聖誕節氣氛的

Christmas card　聖誕卡

Christmas dinner　聖誕晚餐

Christmas Day　聖誕節（12月25日）

Christmas carol　聖誕頌歌：狄更斯有一短篇小說，即以此為名。

Boxing Day　盒日：英國風俗，聖誕節第二天（12月26日），居民住家給僕人、清潔工、送報人、送牛奶工人、郵差等人的賞錢，因為是裝在盒子裡給的，故名 Christmas box，這天亦稱 Boxing Day。

Christmas stocking　聖誕襪：兒童在聖誕前夕掛於壁爐架上，供聖誕老人裝禮物之用。

Christmas tree　聖誕樹：作為聖誕節的裝飾，流行於全世界（伊斯蘭國家除外），其起源可追溯至羅馬帝國時代。古羅馬人每年12月17日至24日，為了慶祝農神（Saturn）節，盡情狂歡，並在會堂中裝飾綠色植物。

Christmas comes but once a year. 聖誕節一年只有一次。（亦即人們應在聖誕節幫助窮人。）

After Christmas comes Lent. 過了聖誕節就是四旬齋。（喻盡情歡樂後要過一段清苦日子。）

He has eaten many a Christmas pie. 他吃過許多聖誕餅。（表年事已高。）

重新做人
A Retrieved Reformation

# In the prison

## CD★26

Narrator：Look out! Look out! Look out for Jimmy Valentine. Suave, debonair, beautifully dressed—Jimmy Valentine's a bank robber. He was created almost 100 years ago by O. Henry, one of America's favorite storytellers. Now, this is the tale of Jimmy's last days as a crook.

Narrator：You recall that O. Henry was noted for surprise endings to his stories? See if you can guess the end of this one. It's the early 1900's. We're in a cell block in the Indiana State Prison.

Guard：All right, Valentine, the warden wants to see ya.

Jimmy Valentine：About time.

Guard：I'm hearing you're sprung.

Jimmy Valentine：Is that what you're hearing?

Guard：You won't be makin' no more of them prison shoes.

# 在監獄裡

CD★26

旁白：小心！小心！小心吉米．華倫泰——溫文有禮，衣著得體。吉米．華倫泰是銀行搶匪，他是美國最受歡迎的小說家之一——歐亨利，在差不多一百年前創造出來的人物。這個故事是關於吉米做壞人的最後一段日子。

旁白：你還記得歐亨利的小說以驚奇作為結尾的著名手法嗎？試試看，你是否能猜到這個故事的結局？時間是一九〇〇年代初期，地點在印第安那州立監獄的囚房區。

警衛：「好了，華倫泰，典獄長要召見你。」

吉米．華倫泰：「是時候了。」

警衛：「我聽說你要出獄了。」

吉米．華倫泰：「你真的這麼聽說了？」

警衛：「你不必再縫監獄的鞋子了。」

Look out! 小心！
suave (*adj.*) 舉止優雅的
debonair (*adj.*) 溫文有禮的
robber (*n.*) 搶匪
favorite (*adj.*) 最喜愛的
storyteller (*n.*) 說故事的人、小說家
crook (*n.*) 惡棍、騙徒
recall (*v.*) 回想、想起
noted (*adj.*) 知名的、著名的
cell (*n.*) 牢房
block (*n.*) 區
warden (*n.*) 典獄長
spring (*v.*) 獲釋、出獄（過去式及過去分詞：sprang, sprung）

Jimmy Valentine：I didn't mind the work. I got pretty good at it.

Guard：Ten to one you'll be back at that sewing machine in a year.

Jimmy Valentine：Not me.

Guard：Here we are.

【knock on the warden's door】

吉米．華倫泰：「我不介意做鞋子，而且我也很拿手呢。」

警衛：「我敢說，不到一年你就會再回牢裡來。」

吉米．華倫泰：「我才不會。」

警衛：「我們到了。」

【敲典獄長的房門】

ten to one 十之八九
sewing machine 縫紉機

# A pardon

*CD★27*

Guard：Here's the prisoner, sir.

Warden：Oh, Valentine, I've got a pardon here from the governor. Don't know what the man's thinking of.

Jimmy Valentine：The governor's a friend of a friend of mine.

Warden：Oh, must be a good friend. Ten months out for a four-year sentence for bank robbery, and you're out.

Jimmy Valentine：I was railroaded.

Warden：Yeah, that job in Kokomo?

Jimmy Valentine：Ko-ko-mo? Warden, I was never in Kokomo in my life. Can't even pronounce it.

Warden：Here's your paper. You're entitled to a suit of clothes and five dollars.

# 一張赦免狀

## CD★27

警衛：「囚犯帶來了，典獄長。」

典獄長：「哦，華倫泰，我這裡有一張州長簽署的赦免狀，不知道他究竟在想什麼。」

吉米・華倫泰：「州長是我朋友的朋友。」

典獄長：「哦，想必是交情很好的朋友。銀行搶案判四年徒刑，才關了十個月就釋放了。」

吉米・華倫泰：「我是被誣陷入獄的。」

典獄長：「那麼，科可摩的那件案子呢？」

吉米・華倫泰：「科—可—摩？典獄長，我這輩子從沒在科可摩待過，連怎麼唸都不知道。」

典獄長：「這是你的赦免狀。你可以拿到一套衣服和五塊錢。」

prisoner (*n.*) 囚犯
pardon (*n.*) 赦免狀
governor (*n.*) 州長
sentence (*n.*) 刑期
robbery (*n.*) 搶案、劫案
railroad (*v.*) 未經公平審判而定罪、將(嫌犯)以不實罪名定罪
pronounce (*v.*) 發音
entitle (*v.*) 給予權利、使有資格
a suit of 一套

Jimmy Valentine：What happened to the tailor-made suit I was wearing when I came in here?

Warden：That－that was confiscated.

Jimmy Valentine：I hope it fits you, warden. And, and thank the State of Indiana for the suit and the fiver.

Warden：You ought to watch your tongue, Valentine. You'll be back here one of these days. Mark my words.

吉米・華倫泰：「我剛進來時穿的那套訂作的西裝呢？」

典獄長：「那套——那已經被沒收了。」

吉米・華倫泰：「希望你穿起來合身，典獄長。在此感謝印第安那州政府贈送的衣服和五元鈔票。」

典獄長：「留意你的那張嘴巴，華倫泰。我敢說，總有一天你還會再回來。」

tailor-made suit
量身訂作的西裝
confiscate（*v.*）
把…充公、沒收
fit（*v.*）適合
fiver（*n.*）五美元鈔票
tongue（*n.*）舌
mark my words
注意聽我說的話（意即我說的會是對的）

# In the bar

## CD★28

【laughing and shouting at a bar】

Jimmy Valentine：Hello, Mike. That's another round on me.

Mike the Bartender：Hey, Jimmy! Wait a minute. Duley, come over here.

Duley：When did you get to town?

Jimmy Valentine：Just got off the train.

Mike the Bartender：Duley, take the bar. I'll be in the back room. Come on, Jimmy. Let me look at you. You don't look too bad for ten months in the 'stir'.

Jimmy Valentine：I was hoping it wouldn't be that long.

Mike the Bartender：Oh, Jimmy, you won't believe how tough it is getting things to work out with the governor. He's getting independent; he's forgotten who got him elected. Your room upstairs, by the way, is just the way you left it.

# 在酒吧裡

## CD★28

round（*n.*）
（酒的）一巡
stir（*n.*）監獄
tough（*adj.*）
費力的、難辦的
independent（*adj.*）
獨立的、不受控制的
elect（*v.*）當選
upstairs（*adj.*）樓上的

【酒吧裡的笑鬧聲】

吉米．華倫泰：「哈囉，麥克，再來一杯——」

酒保麥克：「嗨，吉米！等等。杜易，過來一下。」

杜易：「你什麼時候進城來的？」

吉米．華倫泰：「剛下火車。」

酒保麥克：「杜易，幫我看一下酒吧，我到後面去。來吧，吉米，讓我瞧瞧你，蹲了十個月的監牢，你看來還不差嘛！」

吉米．華倫泰：「我以為很快就會放出來了。」

酒保麥克：「哦，吉米，說來你不會相信，州長現在很難搞，他越來越不把人放在眼裡，也不想想當初是誰讓他當選的。樓上你的房間一切依舊，就像你離去時那樣。」

Jimmy Valentine：Good, I wanna get out of these prison duds.

Mike the Bartender：They sure don't suit you. Here, here have a nip.

Jimmy Valentine：You know, Mike, I never touch the hard stuff. My suitcase up there?

Mike the Bartender：Oh, everything's there, just the way you left it when they picked you up.

Jimmy Valentine：I wouldn't wanna lose those tools.

鎮上酒吧。

吉米・華倫泰：「太好了，我想換掉這一身牢房的破爛衣服。」

酒保麥克：「穿在你身上太不合適了。來，喝一杯。」

吉米・華倫泰：「你知道的，麥克，我向來不喝烈酒。我的手提箱也在上面吧？」

酒保麥克：「哦，所有的東西都還在，跟你被抓時一樣原封不動。」

吉米・華倫泰：「我可不想丟了那些工具。」

duds (*n.*) 衣服
nip (*n.*) 一杯、少量
hard stuff 烈酒
suitcase (*n.*) 手提箱

鎮上的酒吧兼賣雜貨。

Mike the Bartender：Sure you wouldn't. That's a big investment.

Jimmy Valentine：Over a thousand dollars.

Mike the Bartender：And, and you're going back to work right away, huh?

Jimmy Valentine：Why, Mike, how can you think such a thing? I am here representing the New York Amalgamated Short Snap Biscuit Cracker and Frazzled Wheat Company.

Mike the Bartender：Oh, you're a card you are. But getting serious.

Jimmy Valentine：I don't know, Mike. That's the first time I've done time, and I don't like it. I don't plan to do anymore.

Mike the Bartender：But you're the best there is, Jimmy. No one, I say no one can crack a safe like you can.

Jimmy Valentine：Yeah, I know, I know. Is that cop still around?

酒保麥克：「當然囉，那可是一筆大投資。」

吉米・華倫泰：「超過一千塊。」

酒保麥克：「你要馬上重操舊業，唔？」

吉米・華倫泰：「哈哈，什麼話！麥克，你怎麼會有這個想法？我是紐約鬆脆餅乾和碎麥聯合公司的代表。」

酒保麥克：「哈哈，哦，你這個傢伙。不過，說正經的……」

吉米・華倫泰：「我不知道，麥克，這是我第一次坐牢，我不喜歡。我打算洗手不幹了。」

酒保麥克：「可是，你是頂尖好手，吉米。沒有一個人，我敢說沒有一個人比你更會撬保險櫃。」

吉米・華倫泰：「呀，我曉得，我當然曉得。那個警察還管這一區嗎？」

investment（*n.*）投資
why（*interj.*）
什麼！什麼話！
represent（*v.*）代表
amalgamated（*adj.*）
聯合的
short（*adj.*）
油酥的、鬆脆的
snap（*n.*）脆餅乾
biscuit（*n.*）餅乾
cracker（*n.*）薄脆餅乾
frazzled（*adj.*）【口語】
磨損了的
wheat（*n.*）小麥
card（*n.*）
特殊人物、傢伙
do time 坐牢、服刑
（過去式及過去分詞：did time, done time）
crack（*v.*）【口語】
撬開
safe（*n.*）
保險櫃、保險箱
cop（*n.*）【口語】警察

Mike the Bartender：The captain? Ben Price?

Jimmy Valentine：Yeah.

Mike the Bartender：Oh, he's still around. He's a big man now. He got promoted while you was(註) in the pokey.

Jimmy Valentine：So?

Mike the Bartender：He's the head man now, the commissioner. He was in here yesterday for a beer. Asked after ya.

Jimmy Valentine：What did he want to know?

夜黑風高，有人潛入銀行，撬開保險櫃，偷走一大筆錢。

酒保麥克：「你說的是隊長？班・普萊斯？」

吉米・華倫泰：「就是他。」

酒保麥克：「哦，這一區還是歸他管。他現在是大人物了，在你蹲牢房的時候，他升官了。」

吉米・華倫泰：「那又怎樣？」

酒保麥克：「他現在是頭頭了，升了局長。昨天他還來這喝啤酒，打聽你的事呢！」

吉米・華倫泰：「他想打聽什麼？」

這一晚成績可觀，共偷走五千塊美金。

註：正確用語是were，但因此人教育程度不高，犯文法錯誤。

captain（*n.*）隊長
promote（*v.*）提升、擢升
pokey（*n.*）【口語】監獄

# Commissioner Price

*CD★29*

【phone ringing】

Commissioner Price：Commissioner Price speaking. Where? Ellenville? How much did they get? Five thousand? That's a good night's work. Clean as a whistle, eh? All right, we'll get to work on it.

【hangs up the phone】

Commissioner Price：Marvin, come in here!

# 普萊斯局長

*CD★29*

【電話鈴響】

普萊斯局長：「我是局長普萊斯——在哪兒？艾倫維爾？他們偷走多少錢？五千塊？這一晚的成績真是可觀。手法乾淨俐落，毫無線索可尋，嗯？好的，我們會展開調查。」

【掛掉電話】

普萊斯局長：「馬文，請進來！」

commissioner (*n.*)
警察局長
whistle (*n.*)
口哨、吹口哨
Clean as a whistle.
非常清白（指犯案時，完全沒有留下罪證）

# Mail Train

CD★30

Audrey Adams：There he comes; he's early today. Oh, I hope he has a letter from Joe for me.

Mailman：That's mail drop!

Annabel Adams：Yes, and he's got a passenger.

Mailman：This is Elmore. That's where you wanted, hey mister?

Jimmy Valentine：Uh, yes, that's right.

Audrey Adams：Oh, look at him. He's a swell.

Annabel Adams：And he's, well, awfully good looking.

Jimmy Valentine：Good afternoon, Miss. Can you tell me where the hotel is?

# 送郵件火車

passenger (*n.*) 乘客
mister (*n.*)【口語】先生（非用於姓名前）
swell (*n.*)【口語】時髦的人

CD★30

奧黛莉・亞當斯：「他來了，今天他比較早到。哦，我希望他有帶喬的信來。」

送信人：「郵包丟下去！」

安娜貝爾・亞當斯：「應該有的，而且他還載了一個乘客。」

送信人：「艾爾摩到了，嗨，先生，你要在這裡下車吧？」

吉米・華倫泰：「嗯，是的，就是這裡。」

奧黛莉・亞當斯：「哦，瞧這個人，他穿得挺時髦的。」

安娜貝爾・亞當斯：「而且，他——他長得挺帥的。」

吉米・華倫泰：「午安，小姐，妳可以告訴我附近哪裡有旅館嗎？」

Annabel Adams：Well, well...

Audrey Adams：She's trying to say that's the Planters Hotel. Right down the street there across from the bank.

Jimmy Valentine：Thank you, Miss. Elmore is a pretty town. If I'm not being too forward, almost as pretty as some of its inhabitants.

Annabel Adams：Why, what a nice thing for you to say. Are you from Indianapolis?

Jimmy Valentine：No, no. I'm from the East. But I've spent some months in Indiana.

Annabel Adams：Are you going to be here in Elmore long?

Jimmy Valentine：Oh, I'm afraid not. I don't know, might be.

Annabel Adams：Are you going to . . . to stop at the hotel?

Jimmy Valentine：That's my thought.

Annabel Adams：Well, I must go down that way anyhow. You see my father owns the bank just across the street.

Jimmy Valentine：Your father owns the bank?

安娜貝爾・亞當斯：「嗯，嗯⋯⋯」

奧黛莉・亞當斯：「她想跟你說，那兒有一家農民旅館。從這條街走下去，就在銀行的對面。」

forward（*adj.*）唐突的、魯莽的
inhabitant（*n.*）居民
own（*v.*）擁有

吉米・華倫泰：「謝謝妳，小姐。艾爾摩是一個美麗的城鎮。如果妳不覺得我太唐突的話，這個鎮幾乎就像它的居民一樣美麗。」

安娜貝爾・亞當斯：「哇，你真會說好聽的話。你是從印第安那波里斯來的？」

吉米・華倫泰：「不是，不是的，我是從東部來的，不過我在印第安那待過幾個月。」

安娜貝爾・亞當斯：「你打算在艾爾摩久留嗎?」

吉米・華倫泰：「哦，恐怕不行。我不知道，也許吧。」

安娜貝爾・亞當斯：「你要到旅館嗎？」

吉米・華倫泰：「正想去呢。」

安娜貝爾・亞當斯：「啊，我也要走那條路，對街的那家銀行就是我父親開的。」

吉米・華倫泰：「妳的父親開銀行？」

Annabel Adams：Yes.

Jimmy Valentine：Well, I'd be glad of your company. Shall we go?

Annabel Adams：All right. Let me get my bike here, and I'll walk along with you.

Annabel Adams：Goodbye, Audrey.

Audrey Adams：Goodbye, Annabel.

送郵件的火車來了！

安娜貝爾．亞當斯：「是的。」

吉米．華倫泰：「好啊，我很高興有妳同行。我們可以走了嗎？」

安娜貝爾．亞當斯：「可以啊。我去牽自行車，然後跟你一道走。」

安娜貝爾．亞當斯：「再見，奧黛莉。」

奧黛莉．亞當斯：「再見，安娜貝爾。」

bike (*n.*)
自行車、腳踏車

吉米住進鎮上的旅館。

# Elmore Town

CD★31

Jimmy Valentine ：Everything's so up-to-date here in Elmore, a boardwalk and everything.

Annabel Adams ：Audrey's my married sister.

Jimmy Valentine ：But you're not married?

Annabel Adams ：No, waiting for Mr. Right.

Jimmy Valentine ：I'd have bet a hundred dollars you were married. You're much too pretty not to be.

Annabel Adams ：Why, thank you. Are you married?

Jimmy Valentine ：No, no, no, no. I'm a loner.

Annabel Adams ：What do you do? I mean, what kind of work?

# 艾爾摩鎮

## CD★31

吉米・華倫泰：「艾爾摩到處都很現代化，比如說木板人行道，一切都很現代化。」

安娜貝爾・亞當斯：「奧黛莉是我姊姊，她已經結婚了。」

吉米・華倫泰：「可是妳還沒結婚？」

安娜貝爾・亞當斯：「還沒，還在等待真命天子。」

吉米・華倫泰：「我打賭一百塊，妳一定已經嫁人了。妳太漂亮，不可能沒嫁人。」

安娜貝爾・亞當斯：「什麼話！謝謝你的美言。那你結婚了嗎？」

吉米・華倫泰：「沒有，沒有，還沒，還沒有。我是個獨行俠。」

安娜貝爾・亞當斯：「你從事哪一行？我的意思是說，哪種工作？」

up-to-date（*adj.*）現代化的
boardwalk（*n.*）木板人行道
married（*adj.*）已婚的
Mr. Right 真命天子
bet（*v.*）下賭注、打賭（過去式及過去分詞：bet 或 betted）
loner（*n.*）獨來獨往的人

Jimmy Valentine：Eh, what do I do? Well, I've been in several businesses. Now I'm,uh... I'm thinking of opening a shoe store.

Annabel Adams：A shoe store! Oh, we could use a good shoe store in Elmore. There isn't anybody here in that business. We have to buy our shoes at Mr. Barrington's dry goods store, and his selection isn't very good.

Jimmy Valentine：Is that a fact?

Annabel Adams：And if you needed money to open a store, I'd bet my father would lend it to you.

艾爾摩是一個現代化的小鎮。

吉米・華倫泰：「咦，我從事哪一行？啊，我做過好幾個行業，現在的話，我——我打算開一家鞋店。」

安娜貝爾・亞當斯：「鞋店！哦，艾爾摩有必要開一家好的鞋店，這種店一直沒人開，害我們都要到巴靈頓先生的乾貨店裡去買鞋，而他賣的鞋種類又有限，沒得挑。」

吉米・華倫泰：「是真的？」

安娜貝爾・亞當斯：「而且，假如你需要錢開店的話，我父親一定肯借給你。」

dry goods 乾貨
selection (*n.*) 選擇
lend (*v.*) 借、貸

亞當斯先生在鎮上開了一家銀行。

Jimmy Valentine : You think so? That would be very nice of him.

Annabel Adams : Well, here's the bank. I'm going in to see my father for a minute.

Jimmy Valentine : I hope I'll see you again. I don't know your name.

Annabel Adams : I'm Annabel, Annabel Adams. What's your name?

Jimmy Valentine : Ralph D. Spencer.

Annabel Adams : How do you do.

Jimmy Valentine : How do you do.

Annabel Adams : Well, goodbye.

Jimmy Valentine : Goodbye.

吉米・華倫泰：「妳這麼認為？妳父親人真好。」

安娜貝爾・亞當斯：「啊，這裡就是銀行，我要進去看一下我父親。」

吉米・華倫泰：「我希望能夠再見到妳。我還不知道妳的芳名？」

安娜貝爾・亞當斯：「我叫安娜貝爾，安娜貝爾・亞當斯。你叫什麼名字？」

吉米・華倫泰：「雷夫・史賓塞。」

安娜貝爾・亞當斯：「你好！」

吉米・華倫泰：「妳好！」

安娜貝爾・亞當斯：「嗯，再見了。」

吉米・華倫泰：「再見。」

# Mr. Adams

CD★32

Mr. Adams : Hi, young fella. My daughter, Annabel, said you might stop in to see me. Told me about your chat yesterday. She's a forward little minx speaking to a total stranger like that, but I love her just the same. She says you're thinking of opening up a shoe store here in Elmore.

Jimmy Valentine : Well, I'm giving it some thought, Mr. Adams. I just thought I'd stop by and get your opinion about the opportunity here in this town.

Mr. Adams : Opportunity! Why son, you couldn't find a better opportunity anywhere than right here in Elmore. We're going to get a spur from the railroad pretty quick. I predict Elmore will double its population in the next five years.

Jimmy Valentine : You don't say!

# 亞當斯先生

CD★32

亞當斯先生：「嗨，年輕人，我女兒安娜貝爾說你可能會來見我。她告訴我你們昨天聊天的內容。她是個心直口快的小姑娘，居然跟一個完全陌生的人說那些話，不過我還是一樣愛她。她說你想在艾爾摩開一家鞋店。」

吉米．華倫泰：「嗯，我正在考慮，亞當斯先生。我只是順道拜訪，聽聽您的意見，看這個鎮上有什麼商機。」

亞當斯先生：「商機！那還用說，小伙子，你找不到任何地方比艾爾摩更有商機。鐵路支線很快就會通到這裡，我預測未來五年內，艾爾摩的人口將增加一倍。」

吉米．華倫泰：「你說真的！」

fella（*n.*）【俚語】人、傢伙（＝fellow）
chat（*n.*）閒聊
forward（*adj.*）唐突的、魯莽的
minx（*n.*）愛出風頭的姑娘、頑皮的姑娘
opportunity（*n.*）機會
spur（*n.*）鐵路支線
predict（*v.*）預測
population（*n.*）人口

Mr. Adams：Oh, yes, yes, yes, great opportunity here. I'd be glad to arrange a loan for you, if you need money to open your store.

Jimmy Valentine：That's nice of you, Mr. Adams, but I'm pretty well-fixed at the moment.

Mr. Adams：And I own a business block over on Washington Street.That's where everybody shops. There's an empty store there that would be just right for your purposes. You sure you don't need money?

Jimmy Valentine：Well, I never was one to turn down money from a bank.

Mr. Adams：Ha, ha, I like the cut of your jib, young man. I'll set you up in business. And I want you to come to my home, meet my other daughter, Audrey. She and her two lit - tle ones are living with me while her husband is serving with the Army in Cuba. Lost my wife two years ago.

Jimmy Valentine：Oh, I'm sorry.

Mr. Adams：Yep. You come for dinner tonight, and we'll talk about your future here in Elmore.

亞當斯先生：「哦，是的，是的，這裡有很大的商機。如果你需要錢開店的話，我很樂意幫你安排貸款。」

吉米．華倫泰：「亞當斯先生，你人真好，不過目前我還不需要。」

亞當斯先生：「我在華盛頓街擁有幾家店面——那是大家買東西的地方，有間屋子目前是空的，正適合你開店。你確定你不需要貸款？」

吉米．華倫泰：「啊，我從來不會拒絕銀行的錢。」

亞當斯先生：「哈哈，我喜歡你這個個性，年輕人。我可以幫你創業。我想請你到我家裡來，見見我另一個女兒奧黛莉。她先生正在古巴當兵，所以她和她的兩個小孩暫時跟我一起住。我太太在兩年前過世了。」

吉米．華倫泰：「哦，我覺得很難過。」

亞當斯先生：「那這樣，你今晚過來吃晚餐，我們來討論你未來在艾爾摩的發展。」

arrange（*v.*）
安排、準備
loan（*n.*）貸款
at the moment
目前、現在
empty（*adj.*）空的
purpose（*n.*）
目標、目的
turn down 拒絕
set up 創立、設立
yep（*adv.*）
是、好（＝yes）
future（*n.*）
未來、將來

# He recognized Jimmy right away.

*CD★33*

Commissioner Price：I want to talk to you, Mike.

Mike the Bartender：Why sure, Commissioner, anytime, you know that. What can I do for you?

Commissioner Price：Maybe we better go in the back room.

Mike the Bartender：Yeah, you're right. Sure, Commissioner. Duley, Duley, take the bar.

Mike the Bartender：Sit down, Ben.I mean, I can still call you Ben, can't I, Commissioner?

Commissioner Price：That's up to you. What have you heard from your buddy, Jimmy Valentine?

Mike the Bartender：Uh, Jimmy Valentine... Oh, I haven't heard of the boy in months.

Commissioner Price：Is that so? A fellow came into my office the other day, said he'd seen a picture of Valentine in the newspaper.

# 他馬上認出了吉米

buddy (*n.*)
兄弟、夥伴
the other day
前幾天、數日前

CD★33

普萊斯局長：「我有話要找你談談，麥克。」

酒保麥克：「什麼！當然可以，局長，隨時奉陪。有什麼事可以為你效勞嗎？」

普萊斯局長：「我們最好到後面去談。」

酒保麥克：「呀，好的，局長，你說得對。杜易，杜易，幫我看一下吧台。」

酒保麥克：「請坐，班——我說，我還是可以叫你『班』吧？局長。」

普萊斯局長：「隨便你呀。你有你的好兄弟吉米．華倫泰的消息嗎？」

酒保麥克：「嗯，吉米．華倫泰……哦，我已經好幾個月沒有這小子的消息了。」

普萊斯局長：「是這樣嗎？幾天前有個傢伙到局裡來，他說他看到報上登了一張華倫泰的照片。」

Mike the Bartender：Is that a fact now? Probably posing with some socialite, huh?

Commissioner Price：No, it was a mug shot. We asked them to print it. This fellow said he recognized Jimmy right away from the train outside of Ellenville, about six weeks ago. Jimmy said he was thinking of going into the shoe business.

Mike the Bartender：Shoes? Not Jimmy. Why did you put his picture in the newspaper?

Commissioner Price：Because Jimmy got off at Ellenville, and that night someone cracked the bank there. Got away with five thousand dollars. That's why.

酒保麥克：「是真的嗎？不會吧，大概是跟什麼社交名媛一起拍照，嗯？」

普萊斯局長：「不是，那是警方的大頭照，我們要報社登的。這個傢伙說六個星期前，他在艾倫維爾城外的火車上立刻認出了吉米，吉米提到他想從事鞋子方面的生意。」

酒保麥克：「鞋子！那不太像吉米的調調。你為什麼把他的照片登在報上？」

普萊斯局長：「因為吉米在艾倫維爾下了車，當晚就有人撬開了銀行，偷走五千美金，這就是為什麼。」

pose（*v.*）擺姿勢
socialite（*n.*）
社交名媛、社會名流
mug shot 【口語】（尤指警方檔案中的）臉部照片、半身相片
print（*v.*）刊登、印刷
recognize（*v.*）
認出、看出

# Built it up from scratch

*CD★34*

Mr. Adams：I'm glad you came by, Ralph. I wanted to show you around the bank. I'm mighty proud of this place, you know? Built it up from scratch.

Jimmy Valentine：It's a fine looking institution, Mr. Adams.

Mr. Adams：We've been in business for 35 years. We started out in a little one-room building on Jefferson Street, and now look at us!

Jimmy Valentine：You've got a humdinger here.

Mr. Adams：Five employees. Assets over $250,000. This is Bill Gregory, our head teller.

Jimmy Valentine：How do you do, Mr. Gregory?

Mr. Gregory：Pleased to meet you, Mr. Spencer.

# 從一無所有開始

*CD★34*

亞當斯先生：「我很高興你來，雷夫，我帶你參觀這間銀行。你知道嗎？我很引以為傲，這地方從一無所有，發展到今天的規模。」

吉米．華倫泰：「規模看起來很氣派，亞當斯先生。」

亞當斯先生：「我們做這一行已有三十五年！剛開始只是在傑佛森街的一棟單房小建築裡，你看看今天！」

吉米．華倫泰：「您的銀行太棒了。」

亞當斯先生：「五名員工，資產超過二十五萬美金。這位是比爾．葛雷哥利，他是我們的總出納員。」

吉米．華倫泰：「你好，葛雷哥利先生。」

葛雷哥利：「幸會，史賓塞先生。」

from scratch 從頭開始
institution（*n.*）機構
humdinger（*n.*）極好的事物或人
employee（*n.*）受雇人員、員工
assets（*n.*）資產（作此義解時，用複數形）
teller（*n.*）銀行出納員

Mr. Adams：Henderson. McCarthy. And this is our vault. Of course it's a little old...lot of newfangled developments since we put this one in 10 years ago.

Jimmy Valentine：Be a breeze.

Mr. Adams：What's that you say?

Jimmy Valentine：I'm going to...sneeze!

Mr. Adams：God bless you.

Jimmy Valentine：Thank you.

Mr. Adams：Never been broken into. However a banker friend over there in Ellenville was broken into a few weeks ago. Robber got five thousands dollars, so I'm takin' no chances. I've ordered another vault door with all the newest wrinkles. Be here in six months or so they tell me.

Jimmy Valentine：That's sound thinking, Mr. Adams.

亞當斯先生：「這兩位是韓德森、麥卡錫。這裡就是我們的金庫。當然，它有點舊了，十年來，市面上又推出了更多新奇的金庫。」

吉米・華倫泰：「一陣微風就可以把它吹開。」

亞當斯先生：「你說什麼？」

吉米・華倫泰：「我要——打噴嚏了！」

亞當斯先生：「上帝保佑你。」

吉米・華倫泰：「謝謝您。」

亞當斯先生：「從來沒有被撬開過。不過幾個禮拜前，我一個銀行家朋友在艾倫維爾的銀行就被撬開了，搶匪偷走了五千塊錢，所以我不能心存僥倖。我已經訂購了另一座金庫門，具備所有最新的功能，他們告訴我大約要等六個月才能送達。」

吉米・華倫泰：「你的設想很周全，亞當斯先生。」

vault（*n.*）金庫
newfangled（*adj.*）新發明的、新款式的、新奇的
development（*n.*）發展
breeze（*n.*）【口語】輕鬆簡單的工作
sneeze（*v.*）打噴嚏
take chances 碰運氣
wrinkle（*n.*）【口語】獨特創新的發明、技術
sound（*adj.*）健全的、完好的

# The most prosperous merchant in town

## *CD★35*

Annabel Adams：I'm so proud of you, Ralph. What you've done in less than a year is just wonderful.

Jimmy Valentine：I want you to know that I've done it just for you.

鞋店的生意不惡。

# 鎮上最成功的商人

be proud of
感到很驕傲、以…為榮

CD★35

安娜貝爾・亞當斯：「我多麼以你為榮，雷夫。不到一年工夫，你就有了這些成績，實在太棒了。」

吉米・華倫泰：「我要妳明白，我所做的一切都是為了妳。」

店員正在幫客人試穿鞋子。

Annabel Adams：Oh, well...

Jimmy Valentine：Before I met you, I wasn't...wasn't the kind of person you'd want to marry.

Annabel Adams：I can't believe that!

Jimmy Valentine：It doesn't matter; you've given a whole new meaning to my life. I love you, Annabel.

Annabel Adams：And I love you, Ralph— completely. I can't wait to be married; I can't wait for us to start a family. Oh, I'm so proud of you.

Jimmy Valentine：Store's done pretty well.

Annabel Adams：Pretty well? Why, you're one of the most prosperous merchants in town. I was going to keep this a secret.

Jimmy Valentine：What?

Annabel Adams：Well, you know what tomorrow is?

Jimmy Valentine：No, well, let me see. It...

安娜貝爾．亞當斯：「哦，啊！」

吉米．華倫泰：「在我認識妳之前，我不是——不是妳想要結婚的那種對象。」

安娜貝爾．亞當斯：「我不信！」

吉米．華倫泰：「這不要緊；妳給了我人生嶄新的意義。我愛妳，安娜貝爾。」

安娜貝爾．亞當斯：「我全心全意愛著你，雷夫。我多麼想快一點結婚，成立自己的家。哦，我為你感到驕傲。」

吉米．華倫泰：「鞋店的經營情況不錯。」

安娜貝爾．亞當斯：「豈只不錯？什麼話！你是鎮上最成功的商人之一。我本來是要保守這個祕密的。」

吉米．華倫泰：「什麼？」

安娜貝爾．亞當斯：「啊，你知道明天是什麼日子？」

吉米．華倫泰：「不知道，嗯，我看看，明天——」

prosperous（*adj.*）成功的
merchant（*n.*）商人
secret（*n.*）祕密

Annabel Adams：It's the first anniversary of the day you opened the store, silly. And do you know what daddy's going to do?

Jimmy Valentine：What?

Annabel Adams：No, no, I shouldn't tell you. It's a surprise.

Jimmy Valentine：Surprise, huh?

Annabel Adams：Don't worry. Oh, you'll be so pleased.

安娜貝爾・亞當斯：「明天是你開店的周年慶，傻瓜。而且，你知道我爸要怎麼做嗎？」

吉米・華倫泰：「怎麼做？」

安娜貝爾・亞當斯：「不行，不行，我不能告訴你，到時候給你一個驚喜。」

吉米・華倫泰：「驚喜？嗯？」

安娜貝爾・亞當斯：「別擔心。哦，你會很開心的。」

anniversary（*n.*）
周年慶、周年紀念日

# Honest Ralph

CD★36

【music playing, sounds of celebration】

Mr. Adams：All right, Henry, that'll be enough. That's enough, Henry. Ladies and Gentlemen! Ladies and Gentlemen! I've asked the town fathers to erect this speaker stand here in front of Spencer Shoe Store, so that I can make a little speech this afternoon to my friends and neighbors. First, I wanna make an announcement. My daughter Annabel, whom you folks all know, is going to be married two weeks from today, and the lucky fellow who has won her hand, is none other than Ralph D. Spencer.

【cheers】

# 誠實的雷夫

CD★36

erect（*v.*）建造
announcement（*n.*）宣布
folks（*n.*）【口語】人們
none other than 正是、就是

【音樂奏起，眾人喝采】

亞當斯先生：「好了，亨利，這樣夠了。夠了，亨利。各位先生，各位女士，大家好！我要求鎮上的父老幫我在史賓塞鞋店門前建造這座講台，讓我可以跟鄰居朋友們說幾句話。首先，我要宣布一件事，我的女兒安娜貝爾，各位都認識她，兩個星期後的今天她就要結婚了，那個幸運的小伙子正是雷夫・史賓塞。」

【眾人喝采】

Mr. Adams：All right. This, this seems like a good time to announce the wedding date, because today is the first anniversary of a highly successful new business here in Elmore－the greatest little city in Indiana－Ralph D. Spencer Shoe Store. I want to say a few words about Ralph D. Spencer. A finer citizen of this town you could not meet. Honest, right down to the ground; I trust him with the last dollar in my bank. You've heard of 'Honest Abe'? Well, now meet Honest Ralph. I couldn't find a better man to be my son-in-law.

【cheers】

亞當斯先生：「好，這個，這好像是宣布婚禮日期的最佳時刻，因為今天是印第安那州最偉大的小鎮艾爾摩經營非常成功的新店——史賓塞鞋店的周年慶。我想用幾句話來形容雷夫・史賓塞這個人，他是這個鎮上再也找不到的好鎮民。誠實，完全的誠實。我連銀行裡的最後一塊錢都敢交給他。你們都聽過『誠實的林肯』？現在介紹給你們認識『誠實的雷夫』。我打著燈籠也找不到更好的女婿了。」

【眾人喝采】

announce（*v.*）宣布
wedding date 婚禮日期
citizen（*n.*）市民、公民
down to the ground 徹底、完全
hear of 聽到…的事（消息）（過去式及過去分詞：heard of）
Honest Abe 請參考書後解說
son-in-law（*n.*）女婿

# A hot lead

## CD★37

Commissioner Price：Marvin, I think we've got a hot lead.

Officer Marvin：We have?

Commissioner Price：Jimmy Valentine. You know that fellow on the train who identified Jimmy from his picture in the paper?

Officer Marvin：Uh, yeah, I remember.

Commissioner Price：He came by again this morning to tell me he finally remembered the name the fellow told him when they were saying goodbye－Ralph D. Spencer.

Officer Marvin：What good does that do us, boss?

# 一個重要的線索

*CD★37*

lead（*n.*）線索
identify（*v.*）認出

普萊斯局長：「馬文，我想我們掌握了一個很重要的線索。」

馬文警官：「我們掌握了什麼？」

普萊斯局長：「關於吉米．華倫泰的線索。你知道那個傢伙？他從報上登的照片認出火車上的那個人就是吉米。」

馬文警官：「嗯，是的，我記得。」

普萊斯局長：「他今早過來告訴我，他終於想起來他們互相道別時，那人留下的名字——雷夫．史賓塞。」

馬文警官：「那對我們有什麼用，老闆？」

Commissioner Price：Well, you know I've been collecting the names of shoe stores all over the State of Indiana. Here's one in, in a little town called Elmore－Spencer Shoes. Owner: Ralph D. Spencer. I think I'll just mosey out to Elmore.

亞當斯先生的保險櫃有點舊了。

普萊斯局長：「嗯，你曉得我一直在收集印第安那州各地鞋店的店名，在一個叫艾爾摩的小鎮上，有一家『史賓塞鞋店』，店主是雷夫·史賓塞。我想我這就到艾爾摩去看看。」

collect（*v.*）收集
owner（*n.*）物主、所有人
mosey（*v.*）閒蕩、漫步

到底是誰撬開保險箱，普萊斯局長已掌握了重要的線索。

# A letter here from Jimmy Valentine

CD★38

Mike the Bartender：I'll tell you why I sent Duley lookin' for you, Joe. I got a letter here from Jimmy Valentine.

Joe Casper：Yeah? I ain't heard from him in a dog's age. Where is he?

Mike the Bartender：I'll read you the letter I got. Let's see: 'Dear old pal, you haven't heard from me in the past year, and I guess you're wondering what happened to me. Well, Mike, I'm out of the business. Yep, I've gone straight.'

Joe Casper：Gone straight?! The boy's sick!

Mike the Bartender：Oh, there's more, even worse: 'I've opened up a shoe store in a little town I won't tell you the name of. I've met the most beautiful girl in the world, and I'm getting married.'

# 吉米・華倫泰的信

## CD★38

酒保麥克：「喬，我告訴你，我叫杜易把你找來，是因為我收到吉米・華倫泰的一封信。」

喬・凱斯伯：「呀？好些時候沒他的消息了。他現在哪？」

酒保麥克：「我把信唸給你聽，就是這封：『親愛的老友，一年沒跟你連繫了，我想你一定在猜我發生什麼事了。是這樣，麥克，我已經退出江湖，是的，我已經改邪歸正了。』

喬・凱斯伯：「改邪歸正?!這小子未免太噁心了！」

酒保麥克：「哦，接下來要唸的，更糟糕。『我在一個不方便透露名稱的小鎮開了一家鞋店，而且認識一個世上最美麗的女孩，快要結婚了。』

dog's age 長時間
pal（*n.*）
哥兒們、好朋友
wonder（*v.*）
想知道、感到好奇
straight（*adj.*）
誠實的、正大光明的

Joe Casper：Married? Jimmy?

Mike the Bartender：That's what it says:

'In two weeks. And as soon as possible I'm moving to California to get away from Ben Price.'

Mike the Bartender：Now here's the part about you:

'I'm coming to Indianapolis next Wednesday to buy a wedding ring. I'm going to bring the tools with me. You know they're worth a lot. I want you to give them to Joe Casper.'

Joe Casper：Oh, he...he's giving me his tools? It's enough to make a fella cry. A real gentleman—'Gentleman Jimmy'.

Mike the Bartender：'Joe taught me all I know. Will you get in touch with him, and tell him to meet me at your place next Wednesday afternoon? Don't worry about me, Mike. I'm a happy man. I've got a whole new life ahead of me. See you Wednesday. Your pal, Jimmy.'

Mike the Bartender：Oh, for the love of all that's good and holy, can you believe that?

喬・凱斯伯：「吉米要結婚？」

酒保麥克：「信上是這麼說的。

『在兩個星期內結婚。為了躲開班・普萊斯的追捕，我要盡快遷居加州。』

酒保麥克：「現在要唸信中提到你的部分：

『下星期三我要到印第安那波里斯選購結婚戒指，順便會把工具帶來。你知道那值不少錢，我要你把這些工具交給喬・凱斯柏。』

喬・凱斯伯：「哦，他——他要把工具給我？這令人感動得想哭。他真是個紳士——『紳士吉米』。」

酒保麥克：『我所有的本事都是喬傳授的。你可以幫我連絡他嗎？告訴他下個禮拜三下午，我們在你家碰頭。別為我擔心，麥克，我現在很快樂，未來將展開嶄新的人生。下禮拜三見，你的老友吉米。』

酒保麥克：「哦，老天爺，真不敢相信！」

# Breakfast

*CD★39*

Mr. Adams：I'm glad you could come for breakfast, son. You don't mind if I call you son, do you, Ralph? After all...

Jimmy Valentine：No, sir. I'm honored.

Annabel Adams：I'm so happy. Isn't it wonderful, Audrey?

Audrey Adams：It surely is. And now, Daddy, you'll have two married daughters.

Mr. Adams：I wish your mother was here. She'd be so happy. Well, we'd better get on our way.

May ：Ouch! Mommy! Mommy! Tell Billy to stop pulling my hair!

Audrey Adams：Billy, you behave yourself.

# 早 餐

honor (v.) 尊敬、敬重
behave (v.) 守規矩

CD★39

亞當斯先生：「我很高興你能過來吃早餐，兒子。你不介意我叫你兒子吧？雷夫，畢竟——」

吉米．華倫泰：「我怎麼會介意呢，先生，這是我的榮幸。」

安娜貝爾．亞當斯：「我好快樂，一切都很美好，是不是，奧黛莉？」

奧黛莉．亞當斯：「當然囉。爸爸，現在您有兩個女兒嫁出去了。」

亞當斯先生：「我多希望妳們的母親也在，她也會很快樂的。好吧，我們應該上路了。」

梅：「哎呀，媽咪！媽咪！叫比利不要拉我的頭髮！」

奧黛莉．亞當斯：「比利，你給我守規矩。」

Billy ：She started it. I'm going to put her in jail.

Mr. Adams：Billy, behave yourself. Now, first we'll go down to the bank and see the new safe. They finished installing it last evening, Ralph, and we're putting it in operation this morning. I'm very proud of it. And Ralph, I appreciate your advice on the kind of vault door to buy－it's a dandy! Where'd you ever learn so much about that kinda thing?

Jimmy Valentine：When I graduated from college, I went to work for a bank vault company, but it wasn't my line.

Mr. Adams：Well, now you have to get your suitcase if we're gonna take you to the train after we finish at the bank.

Jimmy Valentine：I'll pick it up at the hotel and meet you at the bank.

Mr. Adams：Good. All right everybody. Come on, kids, out of the house, and into the carriage.

比利：「她先挑起的，我要把她關入監牢裡。」

亞當斯先生：「比利，乖一點。雷夫，現在我們先去銀行看新保險櫃，昨晚才安裝好，我們今天早上就會啓用它。我覺得很自豪。雷夫，我感激你提供給我訂購金庫門的寶貴建議——真是極品！你從哪裡知道這麼多相關的知識？」

吉米・華倫泰：「我大學畢業時曾在一家銀行金庫公司上班，不過，那不合我的興趣。」

亞當斯先生：「好了，現在你去拿手提箱，等我們從銀行出來後，載你去搭火車。」

吉米・華倫泰：「我要回旅館去拿，待會兒跟你們在銀行碰頭。」

亞當斯先生：「好的。大家走吧。孩子們，走了，上馬車去。」

install（*v.*）安裝、裝設
operation（*n.*）操作、運作
appreciate（*v.*）感激
advice（*n.*）忠告、指示
dandy（*n.*）【口語】極品、上品
graduate（*v.*）畢業
carriage（*n.*）四人馬車

# Bank vault

*CD★40*

Mr. Adams：Now that's the new vault door back there. I want you all to see it. Gregory, Henderson, McCarthy, come on, I want you to see it, too.

Gregory：Yes, sir.

Mr. Adams：It's still five minutes before we open the doors.

Henderson：Yes, sir.

Mr. Adams：You too, Ralph. You are as responsible as anyone for this improvement to our vault.

Billy ：Granddaddy, could you lock someone up in there?

Mr. Adams：Of course not. This is not for people. It's for money.

May ：But granddaddy, a person could walk right in－like this.

# 銀行金庫

CD★40

亞當斯先生：「新金庫門在後面，你們都過來看看。葛雷哥利、韓德森、麥卡錫，請過來，我要你們也來看看。」

葛雷哥利：「是的，老闆。」

亞當斯先生：「還有五分鐘，我們就要開始營業了。」

韓德森：「是的，老闆。」

亞當斯先生：「你也過來，雷夫。我這次金庫改裝，你跟其他人一樣都有功勞。」

比利：「爺爺，可以把人鎖在裡頭嗎？」

亞當斯先生：「當然不可以。這不是用來鎖人的，這是用來鎖錢的。」

梅：「可是，爺爺，人可以直接走進去呢——就像這樣。」

responsible（*adj.*）
有責任的、應負責的
improvement（*n.*）
改善
granddaddy（*n.*）爺爺
lock ... up
把…鎖起來、把…鎖上

Audrey Adams：Now you stay out of there, May. And Billy, keep your hands off that thing!

Annabel Adams：It looks very, very strong.

亞當斯先生的銀行剛裝設新金庫門，看起來好像非常堅固。

奧黛莉・亞當斯：「你們不要靠近那裡，梅和比利，你們的手不要去碰那東西！」

安娜貝爾・亞當斯：「看起來好像非常堅固。」

keep off 遠離

警察在門外等著。

Jimmy Valentine：It's the best you can buy.

Mr. Adams：Gregory, there's somebody standing at the door out front. See what he wants.

Gregory：Yes, sir.

Mr. Adams：Tell him we don't open till nine o'clock.

Gregory：Yes, sir.

Gregory：Uh, excuse me. Excuse me, sir, may I help you?

Commissioner Price：That's all right; I'm just waiting for a party.

Gregory：But we don't open till nine o clock.

Commissioner Price：I know, but I told him I'd meet him here. See this?

Gregory：The police?!

Commissioner Price：Keep your voice down!

Gregory：Yes, yes, sir.

吉米．華倫泰：「買不到更好的了。」

亞當斯先生：「葛雷哥利，門外站了一個人，你過去問問他有什麼事。」

葛雷哥利：「是的，老闆。」

party（*n.*）人

亞當斯先生：「告訴他，我們要到九點鐘才開始營業。」

葛雷哥利：「是的，老闆。」

葛雷哥利：「這位先生，對不起，請問有什麼事嗎？」

普萊斯局長：「沒事，我只是在等人。」

葛雷哥利：「可是，我們九點鐘才開始營業。」

普萊斯局長：「我曉得，但我跟他約好在這裡碰面。看到沒？」

葛雷哥利：「是警察！」

普萊斯局長：「小聲一點！」

葛雷哥利：「是的，是的，先生。」

# Billy locked his sister in the safe

*CD★41*

Audrey Adams：Oh! Oh, no! No, Billy, what have you done?

Commissioner Price：What's up back there?

Gregory：I don't know, sir, but I'll go see.

Commissioner Price：I'll come with you.

Jimmy Valentine：What's happened?

Billy ：I－I didn't mean to. I was just playing.

Mr. Adams：My grandson locked his sister in the safe.

Gregory：Oh, can't you open it?

Mr. Adams：No! The clock hasn't been wound, and the combination's not set.

Annabel Adams：There has to be a way to open it!

# 比利把姊姊鎖在保險櫃裡

CD★41

奧黛莉・亞當斯：「哦！哦，不！不！比利，你做了什麼事？」

普萊斯局長：「後面發生什麼事？」

葛雷哥利：「我不清楚，先生，我要過去看看。」

普萊斯局長：「我跟你一塊兒去。」

吉米・華倫泰：「發生什麼事？」

比利：「我——我不是故意的，我只是在玩。」

亞當斯先生：「我孫子把他姊姊鎖在保險櫃裡頭。」

葛雷哥利：「啊，你打不開嗎？」

亞當斯先生：「打不開！計時鎖的鐘還沒上發條，密碼也未設定。」

安娜貝爾・亞當斯：「一定有方法可以打開它！」

wind (*v.*) 上發條（過去式及過去分詞：wound, wound）
combination (*n.*) 密碼
set (*v.*) 設定、調整

Mr. Adams：Gregory, get on the phone.

Gregory：Yes, sir.

Mr. Adams：See if there's anyone, Good Lord, there's no one this side of Indianapolis.

Commissioner Price：There's only one man I know who could...

Jimmy Valentine：Hello, Commissioner. Where did you come from?

Commissioner Price：Just dropped by to pay my respects. I was saying...

Jimmy Valentine：Mr. Adams...

Jimmy Valentine：In my suitcase I have some tools that might do the trick.

Mr. Adams：Then try! Good Lord, man, try!

Audrey Adams：Please, do something!

Jimmy Valentine：Annabel, that rose you're wearing on your dress — give it to me, will you?

Annabel Adams：Rose? Of course. Here.

Jimmy Valentine：Thank you. Now give me room, everybody.

亞當斯先生：「葛雷哥利，去打電話。」

葛雷哥利：「是的，老闆。」

亞當斯先生：「看看有沒有人……老天爺，印第安那波里斯這邊找不到一個人能打得開。」

普萊斯局長：「我知道只有一個人能夠——」

吉米・華倫泰：「哈囉，局長，您從哪兒冒出來的？」

普萊斯局長：「只是順道過來問候一下。我說——」

吉米・華倫泰：「亞當斯先生……」

吉米・華倫泰：「我手提箱裡有些工具，也許可以派上用場。」

亞當斯先生：「那你就試試看，老天爺，試試看吧！」

奧黛莉・亞當斯：「拜託，想想辦法吧！」

吉米・華倫泰：「安娜貝爾，把妳衣服上佩戴的那朵玫瑰花給我，好嗎？」

安娜貝爾・亞當斯：「玫瑰？當然好。拿去吧。」

吉米・華倫泰：「謝謝妳。現在請各位讓開點。」

drop by 順道拜訪
pay one's respects 表達問候之意
trick (*n.*) 特殊的技能、竅門
room (*n.*) 空間、地方

# You must be mistaken

*CD★42*

【drilling noises】

Audrey Adams：You've got to save her. You've got to save her!

Gregory：What's he doing?

Mr. Adams：He's drilling through to the tumblers.

Annabel Adams：Oh, Ralph, hurry. Hurry!

Audrey Adams：Do you think he can get her out?

Commissioner：If anyone can, he can.

Jimmy Valentine：There, that should do it.

【sound of vault door opening】

# 你大概認錯人了

CD★42

drill（*v.*）鑽孔
tumbler（*n.*）鎖栓

【鑽孔的雜音】

奧黛莉・亞當斯：「你一定要救她出來，你一定要救她出來！」

葛雷哥利：「他在做什麼？」

亞當斯先生：「他正在鑽孔穿過鎖栓。」

安娜貝爾・亞當斯：「哦，雷夫，趕快，快一點。」

奧黛莉・亞當斯：「你們認為他能把她救出來嗎？」

普萊斯局長：「如果有人能的話，那就是他了。」

吉米・華倫泰：「這樣，應該可以打開了。」

【打開金庫門的聲音】

Audrey Adams：It's coming open. Oh, thank God it's opening!

May ：Mommy! Mommy!

Mr. Adams：It's a miracle.

Audrey Adams：Oh, you poor baby!

Mr. Adams：That's what it is. It's a miracle!

Jimmy Valentine：So, Ben, got around to me at last, huh?

Annabel Adams：Oh, Ralph, you're a hero!

Jimmy Valentine：No, Annabel, no. It can't be. All right, Ben, let's go!

Commissioner Price：Now, now just a minute, Mr. "Spencer." I think you must be mistaken. I never saw you before in my life. I've got the wrong man. Good day, all.

奧黛莉．亞當斯：「快要打開了。哦，感謝老天爺，開了！」

梅：「媽咪！媽咪！」

亞當斯先生：「這是奇蹟！」

奧黛莉．亞當斯：「哦，我可憐的寶貝！」

亞當斯先生：「好了，出來了，這真是奇蹟！」

吉米．華倫泰：「所以，班，你終於找到我了，嗯？」

安娜貝爾．亞當斯：「哦，雷夫，你真了不起！」

吉米．華倫泰：「沒什麼，安娜貝爾，沒什麼，這……根本不是。好吧，班，我們走吧！」

普萊斯局長：「等等，史……史賓塞先生，你大概認錯人了。我從來沒見過你，我把你看成是另一個人。日安，各位。」

miracle（*n.*）奇蹟
at last 最後、終於
hero（*n.*）英雄
now（*adv.*）（用以改變話題或開始某話題）

# "O. Henry twist"

*CD★43*

Narrator：And that's the end of our story; an ending with a real "O. Henry twist".

還好計時鎖的鐘還沒上發條，密碼也未設定。

# 「歐亨利式轉折」

twist（*n.*）曲折、轉折

*CD★43*

旁白：這就是我們的故事結局，以真正的「歐亨利式轉折」作為結尾。

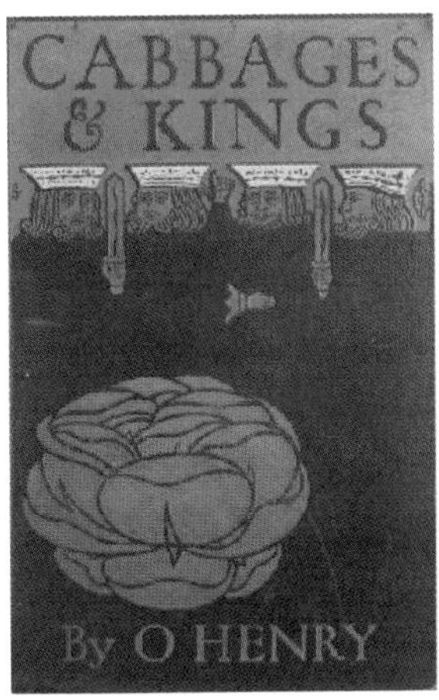


《捲心菜與國王》書封。

《四百萬》書封。

# 〈重新做人〉題目釋疑

〈重新做人〉（A Retrieved Reformation）的題目按字面上翻譯：一個恢復的改革自新的例子。retrieve 的意思和 restore 大致相同，不過，在這裡比 restore 的語氣更為強烈。Retrieve 本來是用於獵犬重新發現一度逃脫了的獵物，而小說中的吉米遇到世上最美麗的女孩，愛上了她，從此決心改邪歸正，隱姓埋名，好好做人。誰知，這時發生了意外，為了救安娜貝爾姊姊的女兒，吉米不得不曝露他撬保險櫃的本事，而特意趕來追捕他的警察普萊斯，看到吉米的見義勇為，大受感動之下，便決定放他一條生路。於是吉米的改邪之心 retrieve，前面加上不定冠詞 a，是表示改邪之心得到恢復的「一個例子」之意。

# 誠實的林肯

英文常出現一句“Honest Abe”，此字從何而來呢？

艾伯（Abe）是男子名「亞伯拉罕」（Abraham）的暱稱。

「誠實的亞伯」（Honest Abe）則指美國第十六任總統林肯（Abraham Lincoln）。

林肯總統年輕時曾經看管一家小店鋪，一晚，打烊以後他結算當天的帳，發現自己多收了顧客幾毛錢。他把店門鎖好，然後走了很長的路，把錢還給了對方。

另一回，林肯賣茶葉給一位婦人，第二天，他發現自己量錯了，少給了她一些茶葉。於是他重新稱適量的茶葉，特地帶去給婦人。那婦人頗感驚訝，因為她根本不知道茶葉少了。

關於林肯做好事的傳聞不少，因此大家都稱呼他「誠實的林肯」。

林肯總統

Studying 系列 +ws

成寒英語有聲書 6——聖誕禮物

編　著—成　寒
內頁插圖—容　容（P028, P048, P072, P076, P108, P112, P113, P116）
副 主 編—莊瑞琳
企　畫—曾秉常
美術編輯—黃昶憲、高鶴倫

總 編 輯—余宜芳
董 事 長—趙政岷
出 版 者—時報文化出版企業股份有限公司
108019台北市和平西路三段二四〇號三樓
發行專線—（〇二）二三〇六—六八四二
讀者服務專線—〇八〇〇—二三一—七〇五・（〇二）二三〇四—七一〇三
讀者服務傳眞—（〇二）二三〇四—六八五八
郵撥—一九三四四七二四時報文化出版公司
信箱—一〇八九九臺北華江橋郵局第九九信箱
時報悅讀網—http://www.readingtimes.com.tw
電子郵件信箱—know@readingtimes.com.tw
印　刷—華展彩色印刷有限公司
初版一刷—二〇〇四年十一月二十二日
二版一刷—二〇〇九年三月十一日
二版十三刷—二〇二三年十二月十九日
定　價—新台幣二三〇元

時報文化出版公司成立於一九七五年，
並於一九九九年股票上櫃公開發行，於二〇〇八年脫離中時集團非屬旺中，
以「尊重智慧與創意的文化事業」爲信念。


成寒英語有聲書. 6. 聖誕禮物 / 成寒編著. -- 初版.
-- 臺北市：時報文化, 2004 [民93]
面；　公分. --（Studying系列；22）

ISBN 978-957-13-4221-4（平裝附光碟片）

1. 英國語言 — 讀本

874.57　　93019997

ISBN 978-957-13-4221-4
Printed in Taiwan